NAVY SEAL HUNKS

NAVY SEAL HUNKS BOOK 1-6

LAURA (L.A.) MARIANI

PEOPLE ALCHEMIST

BOOKS BY LAURA (L.A.)MARIANI

Untamed Hearts

The BAD Boy

The BAD Girl

Holiday Romance

14 Days to Love Series: Short Sweet Steamy

Parisian Serendipity

Venetian Whispers

Mumbay Surprise

Romeo in Rome

New York Melody

Artic Embrace

Santorini Sunsets

Havana Heat

Barcelona Dreams

Marrakesh Magic

Vienna Waltz

Sydney Sparks

Amsterdam Affair

Cape Town Safari

Box Set

14 Days to Love: Short Sweet Steamy

Twelve Days of Christmas Series

A Partridge in a Pear Tree: Hot Spicy Christmas Novella

Two Turtle Doves: Hot Spicy Christmas Novella

Three French Hens: Hot Spicy Christmas Novella

Four Calling Birds: Hot Spicy Christmas Novella

Five Golden Rings: Hot Spicy Christmas Novella

Six Geese a-Laying: Hot Spicy Christmas Novella

Seven Swans a-Swimming: Hot Spicy Christmas Novella

Eight Maids a-Milking: Hot Spicy Christmas Novella

Nine Ladies Dancing: Hot Spicy Christmas Novella

Ten Lords a-Leaping: Hot Spicy Christmas Novella

Eleven Pipers Piping: Hot Spicy Christmas Novella

Twelve Drummers Drumming: Hot Spicy Christmas Novella

Box Set

Twelve Days of Christmas

Shadowbrook Paranormal Series

A Halloween Romance: Enchanted in Shadowbrook

The Midnight Hour: A Halloween Shadowbrook Romance

Navy Seals Hunks Series

SEALed Hearts

SEALed with a Kiss

SEALed Undercover

SEALed Pursuit

SEALed Love Code

SEALed beyond Duty

A Royal Romance Trilogy

A Coronation Weekend Romance

The Wicked Princess

The Lost Kingdom

Box Set

A Royal RomanceTrilogy

The Nine Lives of Gabrielle Series

Gabrielle (prequel/first in series)

For Three She Plays

A New York Adventure

Searching for Goren

Tasting Freedom

For Three She Strays

Paris Toujours Paris

Me Myself and Us

Freedom Over Me

For Three She Stays

London Calling

Back in Your Arms

The Greatest Love

Box Sets

For Three She Plays - Book 1-3

For Three She Strays - Book 4-6

For Three She Stays - Book 7-9

The Nine Lives of Gabrielle Book 1-9 + 3 Bonus stories

Box Set - Italian Edition

Le Nove Vite di Gabrielle: Libri 1-9 + 3 Bonus

Ebook ISBN: 978-1-915501-82-0

FOREWORD

Navy SEAL Hunks is a collection of OTT insta-love steamy romance novellas that are intended for a mature audience. If you crave a fast-paced, passionate read, jump right in!

Navy Seals Hunks Series
SEALed Hearts
SEALed with a Kiss
SEALed Undercover
SEALed Pursuit
SEALed Love Code
SEALed beyond Duty

CONTENTS

SEALED HEARTS

AN ENEMIES TO LOVERS OTT INSTA LOVE
ROMANCE

1

JAKE

The Navy base is bathed in moonlight, and the air stings with chill. Taking a deep breath, I step into the building and head to the briefing room. Mike stands up from his seat as I enter, followed by the rest of my squad, who had already gathered there.

"Hooyah!" I shout, prompting them to respond with the Navy SEAL salute.

"Hooyah! Good to see you again, Sir," they say in unison, each taking their seats.

I take out a folder with detailed plans for our mission while they watch intently.

"Are you all ready for business?" I ask, and one of them nod in agreement.

. . .

"Yes, boss," he replies confidently, his gaze never wavering from mine.

"Feels good to be home, sir," another one adds.

"Good to see you all back on US soil," I say as I settle into my chair at the head of the table.

Mike leans forward in the chair, his deep voice reverberating off the room's bare walls. His gaze is intense and serious as he addresses the squad.

"Alright, let's get down to it," he begins. "As you all know, we had intel of a sleeper terrorist cell in town planning a big hit. Officially, we are here to honor our comrade, Silver Star Captain Armstrong, on the anniversary of his fall in battle and support the locals with the fundraising calendar in his memory between now and Christmas."

I shift my weight uncomfortably in my chair and cross my arms, suppressing a sigh of frustration. It feels like such a waste of time being stuck in this small town pretending to help with fundraising activities when really we are here to prevent a terrorist attack. The cover story seems flimsy, and I don't see how it would help us achieve our mission. But I keep my mouth shut—it wouldn't do for my men to see my feelings.

. . .

"Sounds like a cakewalk," one of the guys, Tyler, smirks from across the table.

"Never underestimate the enemy," Mike warns sternly. "We may be in a small town, but that doesn't mean we let our guard down."

When the meeting ends, I suggest we hit the local watering hole.

"Right," I say, standing up. "Let's show this town what Navy SEALs are made of."

"Hooyah!" They reply in unison.

The streets in town are bustling with locals. I survey the environment like a hawk, striking fear in those who look our way as we make our way to the local watering hole.

As we get inside, I notice her. She is sitting at the end of the bar, and her eyes are scanning the room with an intensity that sends shivers down my spine. Her fiery red hair hang around her porcelain face in loosely woven waves, accentuating her green eyes - which lock onto mine for a second too long as she sips her drink.

It feels like time stops as I take in her curves. She's wearing a low-cut woollen long dress that hugs her body in all the right places, sending electricity through me as I imagine running my hands over them.

. . .

Jessica Rabbit. That's who she reminds me of.

My arousal builds, and even though I try to hide it, I can tell she knows by the mischievous glint in her eye.

I gaze at her from across the room, my feet moving me towards her with their own will. As I get closer, her eyes lock with mine, and a surge of electricity courses through my veins.

"Hey," I murmur, taking in her appearance with a deliberate slowness.

My nostrils fill with the sweet scent of her perfume - white musk and vanilla so tempting I want to take a bite out of her. Inching ever closer, I lean in to whisper in her ear, "You smell amazing."

Her body stiffens, and she turns around to face me, her electric green eyes searching mine.

"This is...nice," I say, gesturing vaguely at the bar.

She snorts scornfully. "Nice? It's a dive bar in the middle of nowhere!"

. . .

I shrug casually. "It has its certain charm, don't you think?"

She scoffs, clearly not impressed. But I can see a hint of something, perhaps a smile playing at the corner of her lips.
Good, I'm making progress.

"What's your name?" I ask, extending my hand.

"None of your business," she says, then walks out.

The corners of my mouth quirk upwards; this town isn't going to be that boring after all.

And you, *Jessica Rabbit*, you are mine.

2

JESSICA

The fluorescent lights of the hospital hallway made my eyes ache as I hurried toward the conference room. Another day, another meeting. At least this is for a good cause - planning the events calendar for the local hero and fundraising for veterans.

I wish the Mayor had not agreed we'd do it in cooperation with Navy Seals; I know he was their comrade, but he is firstly our town hero.

I hate these military men taking over everything. Coming to town like they own it.

Like that arrogant one from last night, the audacity, he even tried to 'smell' me. Tall, dark, muscular, with a strong, firm jaw and uncontrollable cock.

. . .

I smile as I clearly remember his arousal. I walked right off. He deserved it. I HAD to walk away before I embarrassed myself; my panties were getting soaking wet. What is the point anyway? They always move from assignment to assignment, different ports, different women.

I hurry down the hospital corridor, my white sneakers squeaking on the polished floor. I smooth my scrub top and take a deep breath before pushing the conference room door open.

As I enter the room, a group of broad-shouldered men in camouflage uniform turns to look at me. Navy SEALs. I can't help but notice their muscular builds and commanding presence—especially the tall, rugged one with deep dark eyes that seem to stare right through me. Our eyes meet, and an electric current seems to run between us.

Oh, m-y- G-o-d! He is the 'smelling' guy from last night.

"Hi, I'm Jessica. I'll be your main contact for coordinating the events," I say, hoping my voice doesn't betray how flustered I feel.

The SEAL strides towards me and firmly shakes my hand. He's even more powerfully built up close, with chiseled features and intense brown eyes.

"Lieutenant Jake Philips. Good to meet you."

． ． ．

Lieutenant! Jake would have sufficed; what an arrogant prick.

His grip is solid and warm. A little too strong. His huge hand engulfs mine. The contact makes my heart skip a beat. Get it together, Jessica. Arrogant military men are not your type.

"Let's start looking over this calendar, shall we?" I say briskly, pulling my hand from his grasp. I can feel the heat rising. Jake's mouth is curled into a subtle smirk.

Oh, I am sure he knows the effect he has on me, though I'd never admit it out loud.

I show him and his team the full calendar of events and then outline the plan for the charity gala, glancing occasionally at Jake. Each time, his gaze bores into me, making concentrating hard. The man's presence is like a physical force.

Over the next hour, tension rises as we debate logistics.

Jake wants a flashy, daring demonstration and his men involved in everything. I mean e-v-e-r-y-t-h-i-n-g.
    Why do they need to be e-v-e-r-y-w-h-e-r-e?

I push for something more down-to-earth. He is stubborn. So am I.

· · ·

"This is for charity, not showboating," I argue, glaring at him.

He glares back, his chiseled jaw tight.

"This is a big anniversary for a Silver Star. We know how to put on a good show and raise money. Trust us."

God, he is so infuriating. And so damn handsome. I have to keep my composure.

"Fine," I grit out. "We'll try it your way. But I'll be overseeing everything closely and agree with all the arrangements."

The Lieutenant nods, his eyes blazing with challenge. This partnership would be anything but boring. I can feel it already. It is going to be a long road ahead.

After the meeting, I gather my notes, aware of Jake standing nearby.

"This will surely be ... interesting," he says, eyes glinting with humor.

I lift my chin. "It will if we all work together."

. . .

"Yes, ma'am," he says with a mocking smile.

"Let me show the venue for the first event," I say, irritation swirling down my veins.

He is already getting under my skin, but I won't let him distract me. No arrogant Navy SEAL can stop me from doing my job.

3

JAKE

My pulse races as I look at her, and with every minute passing by, my obsession grows. She's stubborn and headstrong, but in a way that excites me. I'm determined to unlock all the secrets of this small town, and she is the one person who can help me get there. But I am consumed by a relentless desire to know everything about her, regardless of the consequences.

To know every single inch of her glorious, soft body.

As we walk through the park, Jessica leads the way to the venue for the charity ball. She looks so stunning. Her wavy red hair frame her perfect face, and her bright green eyes shine with excitement. I try to focus on the task but can't help but be distracted by her beauty.

Jessica, how appropriate, my Jessica Rabbit.

. . .

"So, what do you think?" She asks, turning to face me.

I'm startled back into reality.

I try to hide my admiration as I survey the area. It's a beautiful location, perfect for the event. But my thoughts are elsewhere. I need her to trust me, to let me in, so I can gather information and my men can get involved in as many activities as possible.

"It looks great. I'm sure it'll be a successful event," I reply, trying to sound reasonably enthusiastic.

My heart hammers in my chest as she beams a radiant smile that touches her eyes with pure joy. I force myself to mimic the motion, feeling my lips pull up and my cheeks flush despite my attempts to keep my emotions locked away.

I'm unraveling, losing control, and forgetting why I can't let myself get too invested in her; if I slip up, it could cost me much more than just this mission. My feelings threaten to swallow me whole, blurring my rational judgment and leaving me vulnerable to her intoxicating beauty.

As we continue walking, I notice a man lurking in the shadows, watching us. My heart races with adrenaline. I nudge Jessica to move along.

· · ·

"What's wrong?" she asks, looking concerned.

"Nothing". But I know it's not nothing. I've been trained to spot danger, and that man is a threat. I need to investigate.

"You are acting strange," she continues.

"I think I left my phone in the room. I'll catch up with you later," I lie, hoping she won't question me further.

Without waiting for a response, I turn and speed walk towards the man. I can feel his eyes on me as I approach, and I tense up, ready for anything. But as I turn the corner, the man has disappeared.

I have to tell my team. As I turn to head back to the park, I feel a hand on my shoulder. I turn around to see Jessica looking at me, her expression worried.

"What's going on?" she asks.

"Nothing. Everything's fine," I reply, trying to calm my voice.

She looks at me skeptically, crinkling her nose.

. . .

"Everything is fine," I repeated.

"If you say so. I guess I'll see you later?."

I nod and watch as she walks back towards the venue. I can't let my guard down. I need to stay focused on the mission. But I know it won't be easy. Jessica has already gotten under my skin, and I'm unsure how much longer I can keep my desire in check.

But I have to.

For the safety of the town and the country, I can't let anything distract me from my mission.

As I reach my room, I quickly make contact with my team. They tell me they've already detected some chatter and suspicious activity.

It seems that the town's charity ball might be one of the targets of the terrorist cell.

I can't help but think about Jessica. What will happen to her if the terrorists strike? I need to make sure that she's safe. But how can I do that without telling what is going on?

· · ·

I hear a knock on the door as I lay in bed, going over the plan. I'm immediately on guard, reaching for my gun.

I slowly make my way to the door, thinking about all the possible scenarios that could be waiting for me on the other side. When I finally open it, I'm surprised to find Jessica standing there, looking at me with a mix of concern and curiosity.

"Can I come in?" she asks, biting her lip nervously.

I hesitate for a moment before stepping aside, allowing her to enter. She looks around the room, taking in the sparsely decorated space before turning to face me.

"I know something's going on," she begins, her voice barely above a whisper. "I can feel it. And I know you're hiding something from me."

My heart races as I struggle to come up with a lie, I can't risk telling her everything, but I also can't ignore the doubt that's evident in her voice.

I take a deep breath, trying to calm my nerves. "I am not hiding anything" I say, trying to sound convincing. "I'm just tired."

. . .

Jessica narrows her eyes, clearly not convinced. "Is that all?" she asks, her tone laced with skepticism.

I nod, hoping that she'll drop the subject. But Jessica isn't easily deterred. She takes a step closer to me, her eyes searching mine.

"I don't believe you," she says. "There's something more to this."

I swallow hard, my mind racing. I can't let her find out the truth, but I also don't want to keep lying to her. I take a step back, putting some distance between us.

"Look, Jessica," I say, my voice shaky. "There are things I can't tell you. Things I can't tell anybody."

Jessica eyes me warily, her arms crossed in front of her. "What kind of things?" she asks, her voice softer now.

I shake my head, knowing I can't say too much. "It's just work," I say. "It's complicated and confidential, and I can't talk about it. I don't want you to get caught up in something you shouldn't be involved in." I regretted it as soon as I said it.

Jessica's expression softens, and she takes a step closer to me. Her lips are slightly apart and I can see a pink tongue peaking out, inviting me in.

. . .

I want her. I want her so badly it's almost unbearable. Jessica's body is intoxicating, and I can't help but imagine all the ways I could touch her. But I know I can't let myself get distracted. Not now, not when there's so much at stake.

I take a step back, creating more distance between us. Jessica's eyes widen, and she takes another step closer, her hand reaching out to touch my arm.

I shake my head, feeling the weight of the world on my shoulders and open the door for her.

Jessica's eyes are filled with hurt as she steps back, her hand falling to her side. As she starts walking out of the door, I can't resist the urge.

I charge forwards, seizing her arm and yanking her round to meet me. Our noses practically touch, the heat from our breaths mingling in the tense space between us. My heart pounds wildly in my chest as our eyes lock together.

Without a second thought, my lips find hers hungrily in an impassioned kiss, channeling all of my unspoken emotions into that one moment. My cock is hard and swollen searching for a way in. She stiffens in my arms, pushing against my chest until I release her.

. . .

"I'm sorry," I say then pushing her away, my voice heavy with regret. "It's better if you go". And then she is gone.

What have I done?

4

JESSICA

What was I thinking going into his room? What did I think was going to happen?

But something did happen, bastard! Bastard! How dare he? I am so angry. Most of all, I am angry with myself. I wanted him to want me so badly. His tongue searching for mine made me weep; I felt it trickling down my panties.

Why did he send me away? I could feel his arousal pressing against me.

Bastard! I won't let him see how much he upset me. I won't. Get it together, Jessica. You have always known they are all bastards.

Today, we need to go through the blueprint of the event space. He is so annoying and wants to see everything, know everything, and get involved in everything. And he is acting like nothing happened.

Grrrrrr, I wish I could slap the hell out of him. But still, I can't help but notice how his strong, muscular body shows through his uniform.

"Lieutenant, we should move the stage to the other side, " I say; I can't bear to even say his name.

He looks at me, perplexed. "Really? I thought it looked good where it was," he argues, unwilling to budge. Our eyes lock, and there's a sudden tension between us like a rubber band stretched to its limit.

"I know what I'm doing, Lieutenant," I snap, my anger bubbling to the surface. But he doesn't back down. The stage needs to be where he says.

"Jessica, we've been at this for hours. Give it a rest," he says, harsher than he had ever spoken to me.

"Fine, have it your way," I mutter, turning away from him.

Suddenly, a bang echoes in the next room, shaking the building to its core. Without thinking, I jump into his arms, pressing my body against his.

. . .

"Are you okay?" he whispers. I nod against his shoulder. The heat of his body is undeniable, melting into me until I'm no longer sure where I end, and he begins. I feel my nipples harden and press against his chest, but I don't pull away.

He feels it too, I know he does - as his body is on alert, just like mine. We are both breathing heavily now, and I realize I want him to kiss me more than anything else in the world. I'm like a moth to a flame.

He clamps his jaw and throws me a murderous look. His voice is an icy whisper, "Stay here," he orders. "I'm going to look around and see what's going on."

I nod, my throat stuck in a knot. "Don't move," he adds, his gaze as cold as ice.

I look at him as innocently as I can.

"Promise me," he continues sternly. "Jessica, promise me," he repeats.

"Okay", I agree reluctantly.

"Good," and with that, he disappears.

. . .

Time slowly passes by. I want to follow, but I know I promised him. How long has it been? I can't stay here forever without knowing what is happening.

I decide to take a chance. Cautiously, I open the door to glance down the corridor. The coast is clear. He is standing there, in the middle of the ballroom surveying the area when suddenly he turns back towards me, his eyes fixed firmly on mine.

"I told you not to move," he says.

"I know, but ..."

"No, but," he cuts me off sharply.

"Look, I am not one of your men, okay! You can't tell me what to do!"

"Oh yes, I can!" He fires back with lethal calm. "Now you ..."

Before he finishes speaking, one of his men approaches and calls him away. I try to move, but he gives me a dire look. I inch forward, desperately trying to listen in on their conversation, but they talk so low that their words are lost in the air.

. . .

Without warning, he returns his attention back to me. "You ... go back home ... Now". His voice is very stern.

I am hypnotized and I quickly turn away and go. My home feels empty and cold. I can't stop wondering what the heck is going on. But, most of all, I cannot stop thinking about him and his lips upon mine. I want to feel him. I want to touch him. My body is overwhelmed with the desire to feel his hot breath against my skin.

I slip my hand into my dress and touch my nipples. I sigh as the feeling of his lips against mine floods my senses. I can't stand it any longer; I need to touch myself. I touch myself and imagine his hard cock pressing against me. I am wet with desire, and I am getting wetter by the second.

Ding-Dong ...

Damn, someone is at the door.

5

———————

JAKE

The scaffolding at the venue has collapsed. It was sabotage cleverly and expertly disguised. The danger is getting nearer. And she is right in the tick of it. I need to protect her despite herself.

But first, first, I need to claim her. I can't stand everyone looking at her, flirting with her.

She is mine, no more prancing around. She belongs to me; she is MY Jessica Rabbit.

Mine to protect, mine to fuck.

I find her tiny house at the end of the main road and ring the bell.

It's dark inside. Where is she? I told her to go home.

• • •

I ring again. And then the door opens; Jessica stands there, flustered.

"Are you okay? What happened?" no time for pleasantry; if something happened, I need to know.

"No, no, I am okay," she replies, almost out of breath. "What are you doing here? What happened at the venue?"

"Later." Jessica looks at me, puzzled. "Later," I repeat. "There are more important things right now."

"What ..."

I close the door behind me and move closer and closer. She walks backward towards the couch.

"Now, young lady, you are going to go down on your knees and submit to me."

Her bright green eyes widen, and her juicy lips part slightly.

"Now! On the couch, on your knees. Show me that glorious ass."

. . .

Her breathing is heavy, her eyes glisten, and then she turns.

"Spread your legs."

She is on her knees, her legs apart. I pull her dress up to her waist and yank her panties to the side.

I slap her cheeks gently.

"Mhm …"

"I can't hear you."

"Yes."

I slap again, harder. I run a finger along the slit of her pussy, already swollen with desire. I push a finger inside, and she moans as it slides in. I push another finger in, going deeper until I feel she is ready for me. I push a third finger, shoving it in, so now all three of my fingers are plunged into her pussy, and I can feel her walls squeezing my fingers. With my other hand, I squeeze her tits and play with her nipples.

"Call my name Jessica, call my name."

"Jake."

. . .

"Again."

"Jake!"

"Louder."

"J-A-K-E!!!"

I slap her butt cheeks with my hard cock.

"I need you to fuck me," she screams, finally.

"What?" I ask.

"I can't take it anymore. I need you to fuck me," she repeats, her pussy wet with desire, and I am desperate to have my rock-hard cock inside her.

"I don't know what you are saying," my eyes fixed firmly on her.

"This isn't fair," she says. I watch her hungrily and say nothing. Her pussy is ready.

. . .

I push her dress over her head completely to finally see her soft, curvy body in its full glory. Her bra is barely containing those glorious tits. I now push four of my fingers inside her while moving my thumb around her asshole.

"Ahh …"

"What do you want now?"

"Fuck me please," she pauses, "fuck me, fuck me now, fuck me hard, fuck me with that big cock, I want you so much, fuck me now … pleeeeeease."

She is so wet, her pussy dripping with need. "I want it," she cries. "I want you so much, Jake!"

I whip a condom out of my pocket and slip it on my hard cock, and then I drive it in one stroke to the hilt.

"Oh my God!" Jessica screams louder. Her body rocks back and forth under the power of my thrusts.

I grab her hair, pulling it, as I continue to fuck her, pushing in deeper. Her moans echo through the house. I grab her tits. She raises herself up, and my cock slides out of her pussy.

•   •   •

"God Jake, fuck me harder," she is moaning, screaming, calling my name. She is begging for me; she wants me, and I give her all of me. I push deep inside of her, hard, deeper, faster, and faster.

"This is what you want, isn't it?" I ask her.

"Yes, yes, yes," I feel her pussy tighten, her muscles contract, pulsating around my hard cock.

She is on the floor now, on all fours, and I am driving into her from behind again. I can feel her wonderful ass slap against me as I drive myself in and out of her. She wants more; she wants everything I have. She wants me to take her harder, to fuck her like a slut.

My gorgeous rabbit.

My hard cock is plowing her pussy without mercy, penetrating her deep and deeper. She is barely able to cope with the intensity of pleasure and pain.

"Yes, yes, I am coming," she screams as her cum erupts. Her pussy is so tight, and I feel my cock pulsating as it is ready to come.

I pull it out of her and rip the condom off, ready to come all over her ass. I am so close, so close. I let the first spurt of hot cum splatter over her cheeks. Then another spurt and another. And then my cock is completely spent. I fall exhausted over her, holding her tight.

"You are mine Jessica. Mine!" I whisper "And I am yours!"

6

JESSICA

I wake up to an empty bed, the spot beside me cold and void of Jake's warmth. The soft morning light filters through the curtains, casting a dreamy glow over the room. I sit up, pulling the sheets around me, the memory of last night still tingling on my skin. My heart sinks as I realize he's gone without even saying goodbye.

"Jake?" I call out hesitantly, but there's no answer.

I throw on my robe and slip my feet into my slippers before entering the living room. My heart sinks as I find a hastily scribbled note on the kitchen counter.

"Jessica, I'm sorry. I had to leave. See you later at the venue - Jake."

. . .

A frown creases my brow as I read his words. What could be so important that he'd leave without saying goodbye?

As I stand in the kitchen, I can't help but feel a sense of unease creeping over me. What is he keeping from me? I grab a cup of coffee, sipping it slowly.

I make my way to the venue. I need to find out what happened yesterday and make sure all the arrangements for the charity ball are going as planned.

Jake is already there.

"Jake," my voice comes out barely above a whisper.

"Jessica." He crosses the room in two strides, towering over me. The familiar scent of him fills my nostrils. "I'm sorry I left you like that."

"Jake, I –" I begin to say, but he interrupts me.

"Jessica, the scaffolding for the stage has been repaired. My entire squad is here to help as well reinforcement from the base," swiftly taking charge.

"Jake," I murmur, trying to get closer, "you can tell me anything. Do you trust me?"

· · ·

"Of course I do," he says, his voice cracking.

I can't help but think he is hiding something.

We continue going over the arrangements for the ball tomorrow, not sparing any detail. Still, the tension between us grows, fueled by unspoken words and secrets. As night falls, we stand in the empty ballroom, surrounded by decorations and festive banners.

"Jake, are you on a mission right now?" I snap, unable to contain my frustration any longer.

"Jessica, you know I can't!" he shouts back, his anger mirroring mine.

"Then how am I supposed to trust you?"

"Dammit, Jessica!" Jake grabs my shoulders, his piercing gaze locking onto mine. "I want you! I want you desperately, but there are some things I can't share!"

"Then maybe we shouldn't be together!" The words tumble out of my mouth before I can stop them.

· · ·

"Is that what you really want?" he asks, his voice barely a whisper.

I hesitate, my heart pounding in my chest. "No," I admit, suddenly feeling vulnerable. "But it hurts, Jake."

Jake's expression softens, and he pulls me into his arms. "I know, Jessica. And I'm sorry. I don't mean to hurt you. But I promise you, everything will make sense soon."

I bury my face in his chest, feeling a sense of relief wash over me.

Jake holds me tightly, his fingers trailing gently down my back. "Thank you, Jessica. I promise you, I'll make it up to you."

7

JAKE

The day of the ball is finally here.

I am up at the crack of dawn and head over to the venue, a large building next to the house where Captain Armstrong grew up in, just at the edge of the park. My squad has been here all night, sweeping every inch of the structure for explosives, looking for signs that someone might try to ruin the party.

"Morning, Sir," Mike greets me.

"Morning, Mike."

The chatter has quieted down entirely. Everything feels so odd; this town is too small to make a splash for terrorists and hardly anybody knows about this month long celebration outside Captain Armstrong's hometown. Something does not add up. Nevertheless, we need to be alert.

As Jessica enters the room, everyone stops what they are doing and smile in response to her beaming smile. She is wearing an emerald sweater that emphasizes her sparkling green eyes and envelopes her gorgeous breasts. I can't help but feel my heart swell as she walks toward me, but I also feel an unease building inside of me. I want to protect her from whatever we are about to face, but at the same time, I know she has to be here.

"Morning, Ma'am," my team says in unison and turns immediately away. I have cast my gaze over her; the unspoken declaration of ownership burns with an intensity that leaves no room for doubt. She is mine - period.

"Morning," I say softly. "Everything is ready."

"It looks amazing," she replies, "The Mayor is going to be so happy about this."

Oh yes, the Mayor. He is coming along tonight with no protection and has refused an escort. As I don't have enough headaches.

"Why don't you go back home and get ready for later?" I say. "I'll meet you back here."

· · ·

"But ..."

"There is nothing left to do here," I add. I need to discuss the last-minute arrangements with the guys. I don't want her or anyone to hear.

"Okay," she replies, and strangely, without arguing, she walks off.

I wait until she is out of the ballroom before I start talking. Everyone gets their position and duty for the night.

Jessica strides back into the room forty minutes before the guests come, looking like an absolute goddess. I must force myself to use the one-second rule; her appearance can't distract me. My heart races as I desperately attempt to focus on the night ahead.

The guests start to arrive, and everything is going smoothly. The music is playing, the drinks are flowing, and everyone is having a good time. The Mayor will be here soon for the speech. But then I notice something that sends a cold chill down my spine. There's a man in the corner of the room, his eyes trained on Jessica. I recognize him as the same man I had seen in the park a few days ago.

Suddenly, the guests start cheering: the Mayor has arrived.

• • •

I scan the crowd, trying to pick out the man again, but he's nowhere to be seen. I nod to Mike to keep an eye out for anything unusual.

The Mayor makes his way to the stage to give his speech. As he speaks, the crowd quiets down to listen.

Mike gives me a knowing look and nods towards the back of the room. I see a box with a bakery logo, and my heart sinks. He has double-checked the list for the ball, and there is nothing about cake.

I quietly ask Jessica if she has ordered one without my knowledge, but she shakes her head and says, "No, I didn't."

"Okay, wait here," I say.

"What's wrong?" She asks, looking at me inquisitively. I sweetly smile and say, "Just a misunderstanding, baby," trying to calm her worries.

She beams, pleased.

The bakery logo seems genuine, but we can't take risks.

I say to Mike and Tyler, "You two stay here and keep an eye on the Mayor. Guys, with me outside."

. . .

As we exit the building, I stop the boys. We listen carefully for any strange noises or movements, but everything is silent save for the faint strains of the band playing inside.

We must take action before anyone gets hurt. The cake needs to be taken out without incidents. I turn to Derek and ask, "Can you create a water blade that will disrupt whatever is inside without exploding?"

"I can try," he says, jaw set and eyes determined.

"Failure is not an option, SEAL," I reply, my voice steady.

"No, Sir," nodding sharply.

We quickly work together to blast the potential bomb while people inside are blissfully unaware of the danger. Finally, it is done. When I examine the remains, I can see the definite signs of an explosive device that could have taken out the entire block.

This is just the beginning. Whoever has targeted the town is still out there.

EPILOGUE

JESSICA

The charity ball was a great success and everyone had a great time.

Shame that Jake has missed the best of it. But now, we are alone, finally. He slowly leads me to the center of the dance floor in the empty ballroom.

"Can I have this dance?" He asks.

"There is no music Jake," I smile blushing. He looks so handsome in his full dress uniform.

"I can hear angels singing whenever you are near baby," he replies, pulling me close.

"Charmer."

. . .

Our bodies sway together and I can feel the heat rising between us. It's intoxicating, being so close to him, and I can't help but get lost in his eyes. My heart pounds as he pulls me against him, his body heat and strength sending fire through my veins. His lips crash onto mine in a wild, desperate kiss that leaves me breathless and desperate for more.

His fingers trail down my neck as I gasp his name, and the searing path he follows sets my entire body ablaze. Every touch is like an electric shock, leaving me weak in the knees and powerless to resist anymore.

The heat between us swells until it's almost too much to bear, yet still not enough. He looks into my eyes with an intensity that makes me shudder.

His lips crash down on mine again, claiming me in a way that I never thought possible. This time in a more profound and intimate way.

"Jessica," he then says softly, his voice barely audible. "There's something I've been wanting to ask you."

My heartbeat quickens, anticipating what might come next. "Yes?"

"From the moment we met, I knew there was something special between us. You are mine and I am yours, and I don't want to spend another day without you by my side."

· · ·

At his words, a powerful surge of emotion takes over my body. I answer with a passionate kiss that he eagerly returns. His hands ignite me with each touch, and I can feel my control slipping away.

I'm vaguely aware of his voice murmuring my name between kisses, the sound sending a wave of sensation through me like electricity. My fingers curl into his hair as I pull him closer, desperate to be as close to him as possible.

His lips leave a searing path down my neck, and fire rages beneath my skin. Breathless, I whisper his name, and he pauses to look at me—searching for any hesitation, any sign that I want him to stop. But all I can see is Jake, and all I can feel is the need for more.

Suddenly, he stops. I can see him taking a deep long breath before going down on one knee "Will you marry me?" He says looking deeply into my eyes.

Tears spring to my eyes, and I'm momentarily at a loss for words. But my heart knows the answer before my brain can even form the words. "Yes, Jake! A thousand times yes!"

He beams with joy before scooping me into his arms and carrying me through the town all the way to my house.

· · ·

I am his and he is mine. Sealed hearts.

SEALED WITH A KISS

A SECRET BABY SECOND CHANCE ROMANCE

1

MIKE

The fall air wafts through the streets of Thanksville as I step out of my vehicle. The pavement feels hard and slippery against my boots while the sound of a distant engine cuts through the silence. I hesitate, taking in the old sights and smells before walking towards the Town Hall.

Memories of childhood flood me as I pass each familiar landmark – the grocery store where I'd worked as a teenager, the old school playground where I spent many summers running around with friends. My stomach churns with anticipation as I walk closer, my heart pounding.

"Mike!" a voice calls out, pulling me from my thoughts. I turn to see Sarah James, her blonde curly hair cascading down her shoulders like a waterfall, her blue eyes filled with warmth and curiosity.

. . .

"Sarah," I reply, my voice rougher than I intended. She's always had that effect on me, making it hard to find the right words or even breathe properly. She is the last person I want to see again. I want her. I always wanted her. But I couldn't have her; a SEAL life is a lonely life.

Except for that one night.

I steady myself, reminding myself of my mission. Duty first.

"Welcome back," she says, her cheeks flushing a delicate shade of pink. "I didn't know you were coming."

"I'm here for Captain Armstrong," I explain, unable to suppress a grin as Sarah's eyes widen in surprise.

"Of course," she replies, tucking a strand of hair behind her ear. "We can use all the help we can get."

"The head of the town committee didn't seem as pleased as you are," I respond, remembering the conflict and tension between her and my boss.

Sarah rolls her blue eyes. "Oh, Jessica," she responds, "She is okay; she likes to be in charge."

. . .

She leads me into the Town Hall, and I can't help but steal glances at her as we walk. The curve of her hips, the way her dress clings to her body – they have my blood boiling, my muscles tensing with the effort to maintain control.

"So, what's your role in all this?" I ask, forcing my gaze to remain locked on hers.

"I work in the planning department here in the Town Hall ...," she explains, her fingers brushing against mine as she hands me a stack of calendars.

"Makes sense," I nod absently, and my thoughts wander. The attraction between us is undeniable, but I can't afford to let it distract me.

"Mike?" Sarah's voice brings me back to reality, and I realize I've been staring at her for far too long.

"Sorry," I mumble, feeling the heat rise in my cheeks. "My thoughts went just into planning mode."

"Understandable," she says softly, her hand resting on my arm for a moment before pulling away. And with that simple touch, my cock started stirring in my pants, and I hope to God she can't see it.

• • •

I force myself to focus on the task at hand. Still, my mind keeps drifting; the weight of my desire presses against my chest. I can't escape the image of her blue eyes staring back at me when we made love that once.

We start looking at the plans for the parade for Thanksgiving and I can see they have several floats.

"Where do you keep these?"

"Oh, each group looks after their own," she replies innocently. Damn, it's going to be difficult to secure them all without raising suspicion and blow our cover. I bet they never had security before.

I nod, thinking. I want her so badly. "I've missed you," the words slip out of my mouth. *Shit.*

"I've missed you too," she replies softly.

I can't help myself, and I kiss her. She responds eagerly. My cock is pushing against her.
    Shit, shit, shit …

Hastily, I pull away. "I shouldn't have done that. I can't do this, Sarah …." I mutter.

• • •

Mike, what the fuck are you doing?

We continue reviewing the plans for the parade for a few hours when I hear from Lieutenant Philips.

"My boss," I say." I have to go."
    "Sure," she replies, "See you tomorrow?" Her cheeks a deep shade of red.

"Of course!"

As I leave the building, I hear a familiar voice: "Hello, Romeo." It's Ava, Sarah's best friend.

"Hello, Ava," we hurl at each other. She has blossomed into a pixie, Betty Boop. And she has lost none of her sharp wit and quick tongue.

"Thread carefully, Romeo," she warns as she looks into my eyes sternly.

"What do you mean?"

"You know exactly what I mean," Ava replies with fire." If you hurt her, I'll tear your heart out, Seal or not Seal."

• • •

Welcome back home Mike.

2

SARAH

Of all the Navy Seals to come to town, he had to be him. My heart skipped a beat when I saw him walking toward me. His rugged handsomeness is more intense and masculine than before. His rock-hard chest expands under his uniform every time he steps toward me.

We have not seen each other in years, and now we are here, working together. I hope no one else can hear my heart pounding in my chest. Can he feel it? How he looks at me makes it difficult to concentrate on reviewing the parade details with him. Every time I look down at my paper, I lose my place.

As he leans closer to point at something, I catch a whiff of his cologne and the scent of his sweat. That intoxicating smell makes me feel weak in the knees, and I have to steady myself against the table. His voice is deep and commanding, the same voice that used to whisper sweet nothings in my ear.

. . .

I shake my head, trying to clear my thoughts. This is not the time or the place for these feelings. We have a job to do, and I need to focus on that. I have responsibilities now.

But as the day wears on, it becomes increasingly difficult for me to ignore it: the chemistry between us is still there. When he accidentally brushes his hand against mine, I feel a jolt of electricity shooting up my arm. And when we take a break from work to grab a quick lunch, he leans close to me, and I can feel his breath on my neck. I feel my face flush with embarrassment, but he smirks at me.

"You know, you're even more beautiful than I remember," he says, his voice low and husky. "You're not a girl anymore," barely above a whisper. "You've grown into such a beautiful woman."

"I've missed you," he then whispers. I can't believe what I'm hearing. Did he really say that? I can feel my face turning red as I try to hide my excitement. "I've missed you too," I reply, quickly, too quickly.

He comes closer, his eyes fixed on mine. He is firm and reassuring yet gentle at the same time. It's like he knows exactly what I need; I can feel the heat rising between us as if the air around us has suddenly become too thick to breathe. I can't remember the last time I felt this alive. The tension between us is palpable, and I can feel my heart racing. I want him so badly; it hurts.

. . .

'*Stop, Sarah, stop it before it's too late.*' I try to catch my breath '*he mustn't find out ...*"

We sit silently for a few moments, both lost in our thoughts.

"Sarah, I—" he starts, but the words seem to catch in his throat. The next thing I know, his lips are on mine. His kiss is so deep and passionate that it feels like every nerve in my body is alight with a fire that only he can put out. His hands move along my body with purpose, leaving me shaking and longing for more. Oh God!

"*Stop it, Sarah! STOP IT!*" but I can't. I don't want to. Our kisses are hungry and wild, our bodies pressed together, his cock hard pushing against me. I can see the raw need in his eyes, and I know that he knows what I'm feeling.

But just as quickly as it started, he pulls away, his eyes clouded with emotion. "I'm sorry," he murmurs, his voice rough.

I open my mouth to speak, but he cuts me off. "I shouldn't have done that. I can't do this, Sarah. And I'm... well, I'm a Navy Seal. I'm not here for romance or anything like that."

His words cut through me like a knife, and I feel a pang of shame and guilt. He's right, of course. What was I thinking?

3

MIKE

The intercepted chatter indicated that the terrorists were planning an attack against the charity ball tonight.

A few days ago, the scaffolding for the stage suddenly collapsed, and we were confident it was sabotage. No matter how hard we look, the danger is getting closer. We have worked at the venue all night, sweeping every inch of the structure for explosives, looking for signs that someone might try to ruin the party.

Now, the chatter has quieted down entirely. Something does not add up. The boss has called reinforcements from the nearby base. Tonight, we need to be alert; the entire town is here. And Sarah.

There is a small van approaching the backdoor.

. . .

"Delivery," the driver says, "a cake for the ball," and he shows me a delivery note.

I quickly check the list of the suppliers and goods. "You are not on the list!" The instruction on the cake is "For the Mayor to open the celebrations!" I don't like this, I don't like it at all!

I get my men to keep the driver while I contact the boss. He checks that Sarah, the head of the town committee, had not ordered it. The Lieutenant comes out looking tense.

"Boss, what's the plan?" I say, looking at him.

"You two stay here and keep an eye on the Mayor. Guys, with me outside," he barks.

"Understood." I nod. The Mayor, right. But I need to keep my eyes on Sarah, too. I can't let anything happen to her; the thought of losing her is unbearable.

I want her desperately. I have always wanted her. She is the only woman I have ever wanted. And she is mine. She has always been. Even as a skinny kid, I used to beat up everyone and everything that stood between me and her. And now, now, I would rip anyone apart if they tried to hurt her. Limb by limb, bone by bone. She is mine.

Mine to fuck, mine to protect. Mine, mine, mine.

. . .

But I can't let myself get distracted. Not right now; there is too much at stake. I watch her from a distance; I follow her, blending into the shadows. If anything happens, I'll be there in an instant, ready to shield her from any danger.

Keep your eyes on the ball, Mike.

My phone buzzes, and I glance down at the screen. "Done" – the Lieutenant's terse message confirms they have everything under control. They water blasted it, an explosive device that could have taken out the entire block.

I take a deep breath, fighting the urge to run to Sarah and whisk her away into my arms. The charity ball is coming to a close, and people begin to trickle out of the town hall, blissfully unaware of what has just happened.

I keep my eyes on Sarah, ensuring she's not in danger. I exhale a breath I didn't even know I was holding when she steps out into the cool night air.

As the crowds disperse, I can feel my heart pounding as I approach her. She turns to look at me, "Hello there, where have you been all night?" she asks.

I reply softly, breathing in the scent of her hair. "Mingling," feeling a rush of affection wash over me, I can feel my desire for her growing every second, and I know I want her now more than ever. I have to claim her.

I lean down to capture her lips in a searing kiss. She melts into me, her body pressing against mine as I deepen the kiss, my tongue tangling with hers. I pull back, panting with need, and look down at her flushed face. "I want you, Sarah".

She looks up at me with a mix of surprise and desire in her eyes. "I want you too," she whispers, her voice barely audible in the darkness.

Without a second thought, I take her hand and lead her back inside the empty ballroom, pressing her against the brick wall. I claim her lips, my hands roaming over her body, feeling every curve and dip. She moans softly into my mouth, her hands tugging at my chest, urging me to take her.

I know I shouldn't let my personal desires interfere with the mission; we are not out of danger yet, but I can't resist her any longer. I need her too much. I push aside the thought of the potential consequences and give in to the fire burning inside me.

She's mine; I'll do whatever it takes to make her mine forever.

I start caressing her soft breasts through her silky gown, feeling so eager to explore her body. I widen my knees, pressing my aching cock against the soft, plush fabric of her dress. She moans into my mouth as I run one hand down her side, over the curve of her hips, and back up again.

I can't resist any longer, so I swiftly unzip her dress. She smiles shyly up at me as I pull the folds of the dress apart and push it down over her shoulders. She gasps as I yank the dress down to her waist, revealing her lacy black bra. I lean forward and take her dusky nipple between my lips, sucking eagerly. She moans as I roll the sensitive bud between my teeth and then flick it with my tongue. My cock is so hard it hurts, but I love the sensation.

"I want you. I want you so much," Sarah whispers, pulling my dress uniform.

I can feel my cock straining against the front of my pants as I continue toying with her tits, and I know that I have to have her right now. I move my lips down to her neck, kissing and sucking against her soft skin. I press my hips forward, grinding my cock against her. She writhes against me, her body quivering with pleasure as she begins undoing my belt buckle. She gasps as I yank her panties to one side and slip my fingers between her pussy lips. I quickly find her clit and start rubbing it in small circles, smiling at her sexy moan.

"Oh, yes," she moans, pushing her hips against my hand.

She's so fucking wet. I love the sensation. I work her clit faster, my fingers sliding up and down her soft folds. She pants, her breathing growing shallow as she closes her eyes and throws her head back.

"Oh, Mike," she groans, her pussy tightening around my fingers.

"Yeah, that's it," I say, rubbing her clit faster.

She starts grinding against my hand and digs her nails into my shoulder as she moans loudly.

"That's it, baby," I say, rubbing her clit a little faster.

"Please, Mike, I'm so close," she breathes, rolling her hips against my hand.

I work her clit furiously, my cock throbbing with need.

"Oh, yes," she groans, her pussy tightening some more around my fingers. My cock is straining against my pants so much it hurts. Suddenly, she reaches down and slips her fingers under my waistband, rubbing the tip of my cock. I shudder as the sensation washes over me and then yank her hand away.

I unhook her bra and pull it off, baring her large breasts. I growl and push her over one of the tables and pull the dress all the way down, exposing her glorious round ass; my mouth watering as I watch her hungrily, rubbing my cock as I take in the beauty of her round cheeks. I keep rubbing it against her pussy, pressing the tip against her entrance, and then slowly inch the end of my cock inside her.

"Please, Mike," she moaned as I started to pull out.

"I haven't got a condom," *shit shit shit...*

"I'm on the pill," panting heavily, "please don't stop," she begs me.

"Are you sure?"

"Yes, yes, yeeeees!"

I push myself back inside her, and I start to slowly pump her. I love to see her reaction as I push in and pull out of her, smiling as I hear her moaning, getting faster and louder.

"Oh, Mike," she moans, spreading her legs even more. "I want you so much," she sighs, pushing her hips back against me as my cock slips more inside her.

"Oh God!"

. . .

"That's not it, baby, there is more, have you forgotten?" and with that, I plunder my entire hard cock inside her. I can feel her body shudder as I reach her sweet spot.

"Oh my God, Mike, yes," she screams.

I work my cock in and out of her, faster and faster, and she's moaning louder and louder. I have never heard anything so sweet in my life. She screams my name, begging me. She sounds breathless, and I love it.

"Oh, baby, I love fucking you. You feel so good," and I love saying that to her, wishing I were the only one who had been inside her, that she had only been fucked by me.

"Oh, Mike, I'm so close; I'm going to come," with that, she screams my name louder than I have ever heard her scream. I feel her pussy tighten around my cock, and I push even faster into her, savoring the sensation of her body.

"Oh fuck, oh fuck, ohfuckohfuckohfuck"

I pull out and push my cock inside her asshole. She liked it last time. I slip four fingers inside her pussy, and she moans loudly, a mix of pain and pleasure.

She is bucking hard against me. I push my fingers deeper

inside her, and I feel her body moving closer and closer to orgasm.

"Oh, Mike, fuck," she moans, her pussy quivering around my fingers.

I start rubbing my thumb against her clit as I shove my cock faster and harder inside her.

"Oh fuck, oh fuck fuck fuck" she screams, and I can feel her pussy tighten around my fingers as she comes in my hand.

"I'm coming, baby," I scream out, pumping my cock hard into her ass. "You are the only woman I have ever wanted, Sarah," I say, panting heavily, my cum filling her ass.

The table collapses on the floor. I can't think of anything other than holding her, and I know I never want to let her go.

4

———————

MIKE

The last of the sun's rays stream down the town square, bathing the surrounding buildings in a warm orange glow. The streets have emptied out, except for a few stragglers and some locals who eat dinner at their favorite diner.

I stop when I see Mayor Mitchell Jackson approach. He has salt-and-pepper hair above his ears and a bushy mustache that curls under his nose. The man's rocking a long coat that makes him look like a small-town sheriff from the bygone era. Despite his attempt to appear like a friendly, small-town Mayor, nothing can disguise his stern ex-military demeanor. He stops beside me and stares hard into my eyes.

"Mike," the Mayor says, his voice tense. "We need to talk."

"Yes, Sir. " I know the old man is a comrade of our Commander, but boy, he is making it hard for us to do our job. "How can I help Sir?" I ask, feeling my muscles tense with unease.

"Your relationship with Sarah, Sarah James," he replies after a few moments. "I don't think it's wise for you two to be together."

"Excuse me?" My blood begins to boil at his audacity. *How does he know?* "Sir, there is no ...," I start, but he stops me midair.

"Don't lie to me, Leading Petty Officer."

"Sir, with all due respect, Sir, whatever there is between Sarah and me is none of your business, Sir," I try to contain my anger. He looks back at me like he has forgotten this is none of his concern.

"She's been through enough," he adds, his voice softer now that he speaks of her, "She doesn't need more complications."

"Complications?" I scoff. "You really think I'd hurt her?"

"Sarah's a single mother," he reveals, "She needs stability, support, and protection," he continues. "Your life is a hard one, SEAL. Believe me, I know!"

. . .

My heart feels like it's been sucker-punched.

"Does she know you're telling me this?" I ask, finding it hard to breathe.

"Of course not," he sighs. "But I thought you should know before you got too involved."

Too late for that, I mutter under my breath. I need to talk to her. I need to understand. But most of all, I need to make sure she's okay.

5

SARAH

A va snaps her fingers in front of my face, trying to wake me from my trance." Sarah, Sarah .... wakey wakey."

"The sex must have been super freaking amazing," she continues, "I mean after your self-imposed looooong draught."

"A-V-A!"

"Common, it is written all over your face you had sex," my best friend since kindergarten, she knows me well. I blush. It was mind-blowing, and I'm still recovering.

"You have to tell him," Ava urges me, her sparkling brown eyes filled with concern as we sit in her cozy living room. "He deserves to know."

. . .

I look away and take a sip from my mug of steaming tea, feeling the warmth spread through my hands. "I know, but... how do you tell someone they have a child they never knew about? It's not exactly an easy conversation to have."

Ava sighs and crosses her ankles, leaning back into the plush sofa cushions." Maybe not," she concedes, "but it's necessary. You owe it to him and your child, to be honest."

Biting my lip, I nod. She's right. As terrifying as the thought is, I can't keep this from him any longer.

* * *

Mike arrives for our meeting late, a stern look on his face.
"Mike, what's going on?" I ask, worry etched across my face. "You look upset."

He lets out a deep sigh before responding. "I just left a conversation with your friendly Mayor."

"Oh, you did?" My eyebrows furrowed in confusion.

His gaze shifts to the floor, his hands balling into fists at his sides. "He gave me a warning ..." he says, his voice cracking slightly," to stay away from you."

• • •

I can feel my heart racing in my chest. "What?" I reply incredulously.

"Why didn't you tell me, Sarah?" His words seem to hang between us, and I feel like the world is spinning around me.

Oh God, does he know? I wanted to tell him myself.

His eyes are raging with emotions. "Damn it, Sarah! I would have understood," he explodes, his emotions getting the best of him. His big body is pumping with anger; I have never seen him this worked up before.

"What happened to him? Is he still in the picture?" he continues, his voice rising above a whisper. *Okay, he doesn't know ...*

"No, he is not ... "I pause, "He has never been," I confess and feel like a boulder has dropped from my chest.

"He left you? Has the bastard left you on your own?" his anger showing fully.

I continue down the path, trying to figure out how to explain things without hurting him too much or scaring him away. "Let's go for a walk," I say, hoping the fresh air helps calm him.

• • •

When we stop walking and sit under a large oak tree next to a pond and into the silence of nature around us, I look at Mike and say, "There's something else I need to tell you."

His hand reaches over, and he says, "Anything, Sarah," gently squeezing my hands, trying to offer reassurance. "You can tell me anything. Do you want me to kill him?" I don't know if he is joking or not.

I inhale deeply, my lungs expanding with the weight of my words. My breath shudders as I exhale, steadying myself against the gravity of the confession that is about to spill from my lips.

"Is it a boy or a girl?" he then asks.

"I have a daughter," I say quietly, taking another long, deep breath, "We have a daughter." My heart beats erratically, and I brace myself for his reaction.

For a moment, Mike stares at me, his brown eyes wide with shock. His silence feels like an eternity before he finally speaks. "A daughter? We … ? How … ?"

"That night, when we...," I confess, tears prickling at the corners of my eyes. "Apparently, once is more than enough …" Memories flood back: the warmth of Mike's skin under mine, the way his breath hitched in his throat, the rush of adrenaline as we gave in to desire.

. . .

"Why didn't you tell me? Do you have any idea how much this would have changed everything?" The anger in his voice is palpable.

"I know," I whisper brokenly. "I didn't want you to change your plans. You've always wanted to get away from here. To be a Seal and serve our country. I didn't want to take that away from you. You would have hated staying here..." Tears start falling down my cheeks; my heart feels like it's breaking into tiny pieces. "You don't have to worry. Francis and I are fine."

"Sarah," he says, taking my hands in his. "This is my child—our child—I want to be part of her life."

I nod.

"Good," he says, pulling me into his arms.

"Mike," I breathe in, burying my face in his chest.

"Francis ... You called her Francis?" he asks, smiling from ear to ear.

"I wanted her to have something of you ..."

. . .

"Can ... Can I meet her?" he says hesitantly.

"Sure," I reply, a faint smile on my lips. "She'll be home from my sister's place soon."

"What have you told her about me?"

"That her father is a war hero, protecting us and our country from evil."

"Sarah," he says, his voice thick with emotion. "I'm not perfect, but I promise you, I'll do everything in my power to protect you both, to be there for you."

6

MIKE

I *can't believe I have a daughter. Francis ...*

"Michael Francis Thompson," my mother only used my full name when I was in trouble.

Francis. Can I be a good father?

I have never got close to any woman after Sarah ...

"Hey there, princess," I whisper, kneeling beside Sarah, my heart swelling with a feeling so intense and unexpected that it momentarily takes my breath away. She looks at me with those beautiful blue eyes that are so much like her mother's that it hurts to look at them.

. . .

My breath catches in my throat as I realize I would sacrifice everything for this life-sized doll. My little girl. I would do anything to protect her and Sarah.

My girls.

We have to get these bastards. And these bastards have not finished with us yet.

***

"Mike," Lieutenant Jake Philips approaches me, his face hard, "We need to step up security for the Thanksgiving parade. We have managed to foil two attempts, and I don't think it's over yet."

"Understood," I reply, my thoughts drifting to Sarah and our daughter. If something ever happens... I'll kill them all.

"Speaking of the mayor," the boss continues, "We need to increase his security detail. The cake was meant to explode when he cut it."

"The old man has not been exactly cooperative," I say as a cloud passes across my face.

. . .

"I know, which is strange considering he has agreed for us to be here," Philips says.

"Absolutely not," the mayor snaps, his face flushing angrily. His eyes narrow at me, squinting through scrunched-up eyelids. "I won't have protection following everywhere I go," he hurls. "It would scare everyone."

I am angry, so angry ...

"Sir, this isn't just about you," Lieutenant Philips argues. My mind racing with images of Sarah and our daughter. He continues, "It's about the safety of everyone in this town."

"Enough!" Mayor Jackson barks. "I don't want to hear another word about it." As he walks away, my jaw clenches in frustration; his refusal to accept additional security seems reckless. I can't help but wonder if a personal motive is clouding his judgment.

"We need to protect the old man, like it or not." ... *Jessica* ... he then mutters under his breath.

"Agreed," I reply.

"Mike, continue getting involved with the details for the parade; you'll need more men," Lieutenant Philips says. "James, you need to stay close to the Town Hall and the mayor!" he orders before turning on his heels and heading toward his office building.

"Sir, there is no ..." James starts to protest.

Sighing heavily, he barks: "Find a way ... find a way ... you need to stick to him like glue."

"Yes, Sir."

7

___

SARAH

"**M**ike met his daughter for the first time. He took it better than I expected, but he seemed ... distracted," I say while sipping my coffee.

Ava's dark eyes softened with understanding. "It's probably just shock, Sarah. Give him some time to process everything."

Nodding slowly, I look at my watch. "I need to run some errands, but my car's still in the garage."

"Take the Town Hall service car," Ava suggests, her pixie black hair shimmering in the sunlight.

"Are you sure? The mayor uses that car. What if he gets upset?" I ask.

. . .

"Trust me, he's busy all morning. Go ahead and use it," Ava assures her.

"Alright," I agree hesitantly before grabbing the keys and heading out the door.

***

Mike and James arrive at the Town Hall, their SEAL instincts on high alert. Mike's eyes scan the area.

"Hi Ava, where is Sarah?"

"Hello Romeo, she has just gone out," she replies.

"I didn't see her coming in."

"Oh, she has gone with the car, the service car," Ava adds seeing the surprise on his face.

The revelation hit him like a bullet. "She's using the mayor's car?" Mike's chiseled jaw tense. "Stay here, James. I'm going after her."

"Be careful, man," James warned, his green eyes reflecting concern.

.   .   .

"What is going on? Mike! ... Mike!" Ava shouts after him.

Too late.

Mike has jumped into his car and is speeding through the streets in his SUV searching for Sarah, panic clawing at his chest. What if something happens to her ? He couldn't bear the thought of losing her. His heart pounds in his ears, drowning out everything else.

***

The car races forward, the road blurring past in a dizzying array of colors. My grip on the steering wheel tightens as my knuckles turn white with fear. I hear the tell-tale roar of an engine and glance into the rearview mirror to see a black SUV gaining ground quickly.

Beep beep...

I look in the rearview mirror "Mike!"I scream as panic surges through me. The car jerks as it careens wildly out of control, and I fight to stay on the road. I swerve wildly. He speeds and coasts my car, window down.

"The brakes!" I yelled, terrified.

. . .

"Damn it," Mike curses under his breath. Merging onto the road, he positions his SUV in front of my car, attempting to slow me down. If anything is going to stop my car from careening into the canyon, it would be this--if he can get the cars close enough together before I crash.

He is risking his life for me...

From every ounce of strength and skill he possesses, Mike manages to bring both vehicles to a screeching halt... He jumps out of the SUV, rushing to my side.

"Are you okay?" he asks, cradling my face in his hands, relief flooding his veins when he sees that I am safe.

"Mike...," I whisper, tears streaming down my cheeks.

He pulls me into his arms and kisses me deeply, voraciously. I lean into him, wrapping my arms around him, needing to feel every inch of him, letting that passion flow through me. Mike deepens the kiss, his tongue searching, claiming the sweet recesses of my mouth. His hands move down my back, pulling me against him, and I can feel his erection pressing against me. I moan softly as I push against him.

"Sarah...," he whispers his hot breath on my throat and his lips against my skin. My legs tremble, and my body responds to his touch, my pussy becoming wet and my heart racing. "I love you, Sarah. I always have; I never stopped ..."

. . .

I pull back, gasping for breath, and look deeply into his eyes. "I love you too, Mike. There's never been anyone but you," I say.

Mike urges me onto the hood of the car and kisses me hungrily, his hard cock pushing between my legs. "I am here, baby, I am here. I won't let anything or anyone hurt you," he vows.

The brakes had been cut, but whoever was behind this wouldn't get away with it. Not on his watch. I am sure of it.

EPILOGUE
MIKE

The sun dips low in the sky as we sit on the porch, our fingers intertwined, waiting for our daughter to return from deployment. Sarah's blond curly hair catches the golden rays of sunlight, making her eyes sparkle with warmth.

"Can you believe it?" she asks, her voice full of wonder. "Us, together like this."

"Never thought I'd see the day," I admit, my eyes never leaving her face. I squeeze her hand gently, my heart swelling with love for this woman who's changed everything for me.

"Mum! Dad!" Francis calls, running towards us with arms outstretched in her uniform.

"We are so proud of you."
     "Have they been feeding you?" Sarah cries.

. . .

"Mum !!!"

I can't help but laugh.

The night air hums with anticipation as I lie in bed, cradling her body close to mine. Her every touch electrifies my skin and ignites a fire that never dies. The years have not diminished the intensity of my passion, and my longing for her only intensifies with each passing moment. My heart pounds harder than ever before as she draws near, and my cock throbs restlessly, eager to plunge between her legs, in her soft pink pussy and claim her as mine over and over.

"I love you," I whisper in her ear.

She smiles softly, cupping my face with her hands.

"I love you too, baby." I've never feel more whole than when she is in my arms.

SEALED UNDERCOVER

A SPICY OTT INSTALOVE ROMANCE

PROLOGUE

"Mike," Lieutenant Jake Philips says , his face hard, "We need to step up security for the Thanksgiving parade. We have managed to foil two attempts, and I don't think it's over yet."

"We need to protect the old man, like it or not. Mike, continue getting involved with the details for the parade; you'll need more men," he continues. "James, you need to stay close to the Town Hall and the mayor!" he orders before turning on his heels and heading toward his office building.

"Sir, there is no ..." James starts to protest.

Sighing heavily, he barks: "Find a way ... find a way ... you need to stick to him like glue."

"Yes, Sir."

1

JAMES

Mike and I come to a screeching halt in front of the Town Hall, our headlights casting an eerie twilight glow on the weathered brick walls. As we step out of the sleek black sedan, our SEAL instincts kick into high gear. Every muscle in our bodies tenses as we scan the area for potential threats.

"Hey Ava, do you know where Sarah is?" Mike asks impatiently, his eyes darting around for any sign of her.

"Hi Romeo, she just left," Ava replies calmly, not sensing the urgency in Mike's voice.

"What? I didn't see her come in."

"She took the service car; it was parked over there," Ava points to the usual spot for the vehicle across the parking lot.

As soon as he hears this, Mike's jaw clenches. Without another word, he sprints towards the car. Time is of the essence, and Mike knows that Sarah could be in grave danger if he doesn't catch up to her quickly.

"Be careful, man," I warn. While Mike dashes towards the SVU, I take a deep breath and focus on my duty.

"What is going on? Mike! ... Mike!" Ava's voice cuts through the tense atmosphere; her frustration is evident as she tries to comprehend the sudden burst of activity.

As I swivel around, my eyes meet a woman who exudes confidence and strength. Her piercing gaze locks onto mine, and I can sense the intensity in her stare. She is Ava Montgomery, the mayor's right-hand woman.

"Mike's gone to get Sarah; he'll be back soon, nothing to worry about."

Ava scrutinizes me, her dark brown eyes searching for any sign of deception. She stands with one hand on her hip, her other clutching her cell phone tightly. Despite her petite frame, there is a fierce energy emanating from her. Her short black hair frames her face, and her fitted coat accentuates her curves, making her bold and confident appearance reminiscent of Betty Boop.

• • •

"Who are you?" Ava's sharp gaze pierces through me, her dark brown eyes narrowing as she sizes me up. She takes in my crisp Navy SEAL uniform and the stern set of my jaw.

"James Walker," I introduce myself calmly, my eyes meeting hers without flinching. "Here to help with Captain Armstrong's celebrations."

Ava's skeptical expression remains as she studies me, taking in my tall stature and well-built physique. "Another SEAL, huh?" she remarks, her voice dripping with doubt. "And what does that have to do with me?"

"My boss asked me to check out any additional arrangements the Mayor is making for the events," I explain, never breaking eye contact. "Looks like we're stuck together on this one," I conclude with a mischievous wink.

Ava's arms are crossed tightly over her chest, her eyes flashing with irritation as she speaks. "I don't need a babysitter," she grumbles, glaring at me.

"I'd rather be doing anything else right now," I retort, my patience wearing thin as I try to reason with her.

Finally, Ava's expression softens slightly. "So what's going on?" she asks, still guarded but showing a hint of concern. "Why did Mike just run off like that?"

• • •

I pause. Ava scoffs, her anger bubbling to the surface. "Why did Mike just run off without telling me anything? Sarah is my best friend," she shouts.

"Sometimes, "I say, my voice lowering to an intense whisper, "there's no time for explanations. You have to trust your instincts and act. That's what Mike's doing right now."

Ava hesitates, the fire in her eyes replaced by a flicker of uncertainty. She wants to believe me, but she does not trust easily. I understand that feeling all too well.

"Fine. But if anything happens to Sarah..."

"I promise it won't," I reply firmly. "Not with Mike there." I clear my throat, trying to break the tension that has settled between us. "So, how about this weather?" I venture, attempting to lighten the mood.

Ava raises a perfectly groomed eyebrow, lips curving into a hint of a smile. "Trying to charm me, Mr. Walker?" Her tone is teasing, but I detect a slight nervousness in her eyes.

"Would it be so bad if I were?" I counter smoothly, my own grin widening.

"Depends on your intentions," she replies, crossing her arms under her chest. The action unintentionally accentuates her already large breasts, and it takes all my willpower to keep my eyes on her face.

"Nothing but the best," I assure her, my gaze locked onto hers.

"See? That worries me," Ava says, arching an eyebrow playfully. "Should I be flattered or concerned?"

"Definitely flattered," I say, matching her grin. As we make our way through the town hall, I can't help but notice the way Ava's small waist and round hips sway with each step, drawing my eyes like a magnet. I know I can't let myself get distracted - not when lives are at stake - but I can't deny that she is starting to get under my skin.

An uneasy sensation creeps up my spine as I wonder if I am putting her in danger by keeping her close. Every moment spent in her company raises the stakes, and the line between duty and desire becomes increasingly blurred. And that thought sends a shiver down my spine that has nothing to do with the cold.

2

AVA

My heart races as I glimpse the tall, muscular figure in my small office. I can't help but steal a few glances at the Navy SEAL, his disciplined posture and steely gaze drawing me in. I know his type all too well: strong, dedicated, and focused on their mission. But I also see the pain that could come from getting involved with someone like him. My friend Sarah's heart had been shattered before, and I am determined not to make the same mistake.

"Alright, James," I say, clearing my throat and trying to focus on business. "Here are the town events for the next few months." I hand him a stack of papers marked with high-lighted dates and notes. "I've marked the ones you'll need to be aware of."

"Thank you, Ava," James replies, taking the papers and scanning them with practiced ease. "Can I also see the Mayor's schedule? In case we need to get in touch with him." His voice is deep and confident, his chiseled features and rugged charm sending shivers down my spine and making me wet. But I put those thoughts aside, focusing on the task at hand. I raise an eyebrow, my eyes meeting his.

"Why don't you just call me if you need anything? I'm his personal assistant, after all."

James doesn't back down, his gaze never wavering. "I would still like to see it if you don't mind."

"Fine," I sigh, my fingers dancing over the keyboard as I pull up Mayor Jackson's calendar on the computer screen. I can't deny that there is something intriguing about this man, but I refuse to let my guard down around him. I've worked too hard to build my life here in Thanksville, and I am not about to jeopardize it by getting involved with a visiting SEAL.

Suddenly, I see James everywhere I go. He always appears near my office, asking for directions or seeking advice on local hangouts. It's almost as if he's purposely finding reasons to talk to me.

I lean against the doorframe of my cluttered office; James stands before me, his hands tucked casually into his pants pockets. "You don't need to keep checking on me, James," I tell him firmly. "I'm perfectly capable of handling my own work."

. . .

He smiles at me, a warm and charming smile that makes my heart flutter despite my efforts to resist it. "I know you are," he says. "But I enjoy your company, Ava. And I'd like to get to know you better."

His words hit me like a wave, crashing against the walls I've built. The intensity in his eyes is almost too much to bear, and I can feel my resolve weakening under his piercing gaze. "Seriously?" I choke out, trying to maintain a facade of skepticism.

"Absolutely," he confirms, stepping closer until his body heat radiates onto mine. He reaches out to brush a strand of hair behind my ear, sending electric sparks through my body. Suddenly, it feels like we're standing on the edge of a cliff. "Will you go on a date with me?"

I freeze, torn between rationality and the overwhelming urge to say yes. But as James' hand lingers on my face and I drown in the depth of his intense stare, I find myself nodding in surrender. "Okay," I whisper, my heart pounding at the thought of spending more time with him.

A look of relief floods James' face, and I can't help but wonder if I'm making a mistake.

3

JAMES

I stand in the shadows of the dimly lit alley, my heart pounding against my ribcage as I relay the mission update to Lieutenant Philips through my earpiece. "I've managed to gain Ava Montgomery's trust," I whisper, excitement and fear coursing through me simultaneously. She's the mayor's assistant, and getting close to her is our key to staying close to Mayor Jackson.

"Great work, James," Philips' voice crackles in response. "We need to keep this up."

But I can't bring myself to tell him the truth- how tangled and twisted things are quickly becoming. My initial ploy to use Ava as a pawn and play fake boyfriend is evolving into an all-consuming fixation. I can't deny my burning obsession for her now, even though it goes against everything I've been trained for. It haunts me, threatening to consume me and shatter every rule I've ever followed. I try to push these thoughts away and focus on the task.

. . .

"Stay sharp, James," the Lieutenant warns. "This mission is too important for distractions."

"Understood," I reply, though a knot forms in my stomach as I say it. I can't let my feelings compromise the operation. I take a deep breath, pushing down the knot in my stomach. I step out from the shadows and into the crowded town hall meeting.

I spot Ava at the front of the room, her curvy figure accentuated by a fitted black dress that makes my heart skip a beat. She turns to face me, her dark brown eyes lighting up as she sees me.

"James! I'm glad you could make it," she exclaims, her voice warm and inviting.

I force a smile and reply. "Wouldn't miss it." My mind races, struggling to stay focused on the mission while my cock is betraying me.

I quickly assess the room for potential threats as we take our seats. My eyes land on Ava, sitting a few seats beside me. Her red lips move as she speaks, and I cannot look away. I must keep my distance, but it feels impossible when I only want to be closer to her. As the meeting goes on, my mind races imagining what it would be like to taste Ava's lips, to feel her body pressed against mine, fill her tight pussy with my hard cock, squeeze and suck her tits in my mouth...

God, I'm losing it; I'm losing control.

I snap back to reality when I notice a group of three individuals discreetly whispering to each other in the corner. My training kicks in. "Hey, Ava," I say softly. "Do you know those people over there?" I gesture discreetly towards the three individuals who seem out of place.

Ava casually glances over, her brow furrowing as she studies the strangers. "No, I don't think so," she replies, shaking her head. "Why? Is something wrong?"

"Probably nothing," I reassure her, not wanting to make her panic. "They just seem...odd." My mind races through possible scenarios while I maintain a calm exterior.

"Are you alright?" Ava's dark eyes widened with worry as she brushes her hand against my tense jawline. I give her a tight-lipped smile and whisper, "Just need some air."

She nods. As I go to the back of the crowded town hall meeting room, I keep my head low, pretending to scroll through emails on my phone while secretly watching the suspicious group of men.

· · ·

One man stands out to me - his dark, beady eyes darting around the room and his hands constantly fidgeting with a burner phone hidden behind a promotional brochure. I recognize him from somewhere, I can't place where. I quickly snap a photo and send it to the Lieutenant with a text

> Suspicious individual spotted at town hall meeting. Investigate further.

Within minutes, a reply comes through.

> Acknowledged. Stay on alert.

I pocket my phone, my senses on high alert, and then I approach the trio. As I get closer, I can't help but feel a strange pull back toward Ava, a magnetic force that threatens to consume me entirely.

"Excuse me," I say, plastering a friendly smile as I address the group. "I'm sorry to interrupt, but I thought I recognize one of you from somewhere. Do you live around here?"

The strangers exchange wary glances before one of them, a tall man with an unkempt beard, speaks up. "Yeah, we're locals," he says, his voice gruff and unconvincing.

"Really?" I press, trying to gauge their reactions. "Whereabouts? I'm sure I've seen you before."

. . .

"Uh, just outside town," the man replies, shifting uncomfortably. "Anyway, we really need to get going."

"Of course," I nod, stepping aside to let them pass, my gut tighten with suspicion. As I rejoin Ava, she is surrounded by a small group of eager citizens discussing the upcoming events. Her enthusiasm is infectious as she gestures with her hands and laughs at something one of the locals says. I touch her back softly, feeling the softness of her dress and the warmth of her body against mine. For a fleeting moment, I allow myself to imagine pulling her closer but quickly push the thought away.

"Everything okay?" Ava asks, concern etched on her features as she glances up at me while conversing.

"Fine," I reply with a forced smile, mentally berating myself for letting my feelings for Ava cloud my focus. The smell of her perfume fills my senses, and it takes all my willpower to stay composed.

"Great," she responds, unconsciously leaning into me for comfort. "I just worry about you."

I take a deep breath before responding, my voice low and gentle. "Thank you for caring, Ava. But I promise you, everything is under control."

. . .

Inside, my desire for Ava rages. I know I must keep it in check or risk jeopardizing the mission. The crowd begins to disperse, leaving us alone on the steps outside the venue.

"James," Ava's soft whisper tickled my skin as her warm breath brushed against my cheek. Her dark eyes seem to hold a thousand secrets, and for a moment, I feel as if I am drowning in their depths. "Thank you for today," she murmurs, her fingers lightly grazing mine. A jolt of desire shot through me at her touch, my cock hard.

"It's nothing," I reply, trying to keep my voice steady.

Ava's eyes dart to my lips, and I know what is about to happen. My heart races as I braced myself for her next move. Before I can protest or pull away, her lips meet mine in a gentle kiss that sets me on fire. The taste of her mouth and the heat of her body pressed against mine threaten to overwhelm me. I fight against the urge to surrender completely, my hands clenching into fists as I struggle to maintain control. I can't let myself get lost in her embrace, not when so much is at stake.

"Please..." I breathe against her lips, laced with both desire and desperation.

Ava's delicate fingers trace my jawline, but I pull away slightly, my mind reeling. She looks up at me, her eyes filled with concern. "What's wrong, James?" She asks, her brow furrowing in confusion.

. . .

I force a smile and lie, my rough voice betraying me. "Nothing. I just remembered something I need to take care of."

Ava's disappointment is evident as she explodes, "Do you even fancy me? You always seem so distant and never try to get close to me."

"Of course, I fancy you," *baby, if you only knew,* "I am just old fashioned; I like to take things slowly, "I say instead.

I'm obsessed with you. Every single inch of your voluptuous body. I want to fuck you until you beg me to stop.

As we say our goodbyes, the cool evening breeze offers a slight reprieve from the intense heat that still courses through my veins. I know I have to maintain control, for both our sakes. But as I taste the lingering sweetness of Ava's lips on mine, I know I am fighting a losing battle.

4

AVA

As I approach Sarah's desk, I notice her hunched over her computer, her eyes darting anxiously back and forth. "Hey," I say, leaning in close to her ear. "Are you okay?"

Her body tenses at the sound of my voice, and she jumps in her seat as if caught doing something she shouldn't be. She turns to face me, her face flushed with panic. "I... I'm fine," she stammers, avoiding eye contact.

But I know something is wrong. Mike was chasing after her only a few days ago, and now Sarah looks like a deer caught in headlights. "What happened?" I ask, my voice laced with concern.

Sarah fidgets with the hem of her blouse, her fingers shaking slightly. "It's nothing, really," she insists, but I can see the fear in her eyes.

. . .

"Sarah," I say firmly, touching her shoulder. "We've been friends since kindergarten. You know you can trust me. Please tell me what's going on."

She sighs heavily and slumps back in her chair, defeated. "Fine," she says, glancing around to ensure no one else is listening. "But you have to promise not to freak out or tell anyone. Especially not Mike."

"I promise," I assure her, crossing my heart.

With a shaky breath, Sarah begins to explain the situation. I listen intently, knowing she needs someone to confide in and trusting that I can keep her secret safe. "Okay, so..." Sarah's hands tremble as she takes a deep breath and begins to speak. "The car... the brakes weren't working. I don't know how or why, but they just... wouldn't respond. I kept pressing them, and nothing happened. If it wasn't for Mike..." Her voice trails off, her eyes filling with tears.

My heart races as I imagine the terrifying situation. "Thank goodness Mike was there to help you," I whisper.

"Tell me about it," Sarah replies, wiping away her tears with the back of her hand. "He saved my life, Ava. If he hadn't been there..."

I reach out and place a hand on her shoulder. "Have you

reported this to the mayor?" I ask, my mind already spinning with ideas.

Sarah's eyes dart around the room, her fingers tapping nervously against her thigh as she speaks. "I talked to Mike; he's going to handle it. He doesn't want to alert the Mayor yet, but he will dive into the problem and get to the bottom."

I nod, my arm instinctively wrapping around Sarah's shaking shoulders. "Just promise me you'll be careful out there. And don't hesitate to call me if you need anything."

"Thank you, Ava," Sarah sighs, leaning into my embrace. "You're a great friend." I give her a reassuring squeeze.

"Sarah, do you think this could have anything to do with James?" She chews on her bottom lip nervously, my eyes searching for any hint of recognition in her face.

"James? As in James Walker?" Sarah asks, raising an eyebrow in surprise. "Why would you think that?"

I hesitate, but I can't keep it bottled up any longer. "I've been seeing him," I confess quietly. "We've started dating, but he hasn't made a move yet."

"Wait, seriously?" Sarah exclaims, her jaw dropping in shock.

"Wow, I didn't see that one coming. But why might he be involved in my car accident?"

"I don't know…He is ... distant." I sigh, running a hand through my wavy black hair. "He keeps holding back. And I can't help but wonder if there's a connection between his behavior and what happened to you."

Sarah mulls over my words, her brow furrowed in thought. "I don't know, Ava. It seems like a stretch to me. Maybe he's just got something else on his mind or afraid of getting too close."

"Or maybe he knows something we don't," I suggest, my voice barely above a whisper. "He is a Navy SEAL, after all."

"True," Sarah concedes, nodding slowly. "But until you have more information, you shouldn't jump to conclusions. For all we know, the car trouble could be completely unrelated."

I agree reluctantly, my heart heavy with uncertainty.

"Listen," Sarah says softly, squeezing my hand. "You need to talk to James about this. If you're worried, tell him how you feel. He might be able to shed some light on the situation."

"Maybe you're right," I concede, a small smile tugging at the corners of my lips. "I'll talk to him later. Hopefully, he can put my mind at ease."

. . .

"Good luck," Sarah replies, offering a reassuring smile.

"Thanks, Sarah," I say, leaving her desk.

Don't tell the Mayor my ass... What is going on?

I accompanied Tom to the car service just days ago. "Hey, Ava," calls out one of the mechanics from the garage, wiping his grease-stained hands on a rag. "What brings you back here so soon?"

"Hi, Pete," I greet, forcing a smile. "I wanted to ask you about the Mayor's car. It was just serviced, right?"

"Sure was," he answers with a nod. "Gave it a full once-over. Why? Something wrong?"

"Actually, there might be," I admit, biting my lower lip in frustration. "The brakes failed, and if it hadn't been for a friend, there could have been a serious accident."

"Really?" Pete's eyes widened in surprise, genuine concern etched on his face.

. . .

"That's...unexpected. We didn't find anything wrong with the brakes during the inspection."

"Could someone have tampered with them after the service?" I ask, trying to wrap my head around the possibilities.

"Possible, but unlikely," Pete muses, scratching his beard thoughtfully. "We always lock up the cars overnight, and the keys are kept secure. But let me check the security footage. Maybe we missed something."

"Thanks, Pete. I appreciate it." I give him a tight smile, my mind racing with the implications. If someone had indeed tampered with the car, who could it be? And why? As I wait, my thoughts turn to James. Sarah's words echoed in my head - I need to talk to him about my suspicions. But what if my fears are misplaced? I don't want to alienate or think I don't trust him.

"Hmmm, Ava," Pete calls out as he emerges from the garage office, his expression grim. "I checked the footage from the night after the service...and there's a gap."

"A gap?" I echo, my heart pounding in my chest.

"About fifteen minutes where the cameras go dark," he explains, his brow furrowed. "It could be a glitch or something."

. . .

I can feel a chill run down my spine, my mind swirling.

"Thank you, Pete."

5

AVA

My desk is messy, with papers and folders scattered haphazardly across the surface. I nervously tap my fingers on the keyboard as I draft another email to the city council. The steady drone of the heating system fills the quiet office, but I can still hear my heart pounding.

A knock at the door interrupts my thoughts. "Come in," I call out, trying to compose myself. James walks in, his tall frame filling the doorway. My eyes are drawn to his full lips, which curve into a small smile as he greets me.

"Hey, Ava. Can you pull up the blueprint for the town hall and surrounding area? I need to check some measurements," he says.

As I pull up the digital file on my computer, I can't help but wonder why he is asking me specifically for this.

. . .

Trying to focus on the map on my screen, I barely notice as James leans closer, his warm breath brushing against my neck. My cheeks flush and my pulse races as I tried to concentrate. His presence so close to me is distracting but also intoxicating. My mind wanders to what would be like to being held in his strong arms.

I take a deep breath and gesture to the blueprint before us. "Let's start here," I say, trying to keep my voice steady. I can feel James's intense gaze as I explain each landmark's significance. When I mention Sarah and Mike, his eyes flicker with emotion before he quickly composes himself.

"Thanks, Ava," without even looking up. Unable to contain my curiosity any longer, "Did you find out anything about the car?"

James freezes, his jaw tightening as he considers my question. Finally, he straightens up and turns to face me, his expression guarded. "Let's stick to the blueprint for now," he says firmly, not wanting to delve into the topic.

I nod slowly, "Sure," I mumble. "James," I say after a moment of silence, "Is this what you needed information on?"

His response is short and clipped as he stares at the screen before us. I hesitate for a moment before quietly asking, "Are you okay? You seem...distracted." The room falls silent again as we avoid eye contact, the unspoken words hanging heavily between us.

. . .

"Everything's fine," he says, brushing off my concern with a tight smile. "Please, can you print the blueprint off for me? Thanks."

I catch James staring at me as he studies it. His steely green eyes are filled with an intensity that causes a blush to creep up my cheeks. I should have looked away, but instead, I am captured, feeling drawn to him like a moth to a flame.

"James, "my breath hitching in my throat. "I don't know what's happening between us, but..."

"Neither do I," he admits, the raw honesty in his voice sending shivers down my spine. I swallow nervously, my heart pounding .

"I should just...get back to work," James says, though his voice lacks real conviction.

"Right," I agree, his eyes still locked onto mine. The air crackles with tension as our eyes meet, the unspoken desire between us tangible. My heart races in my chest as I struggle to keep cool, but my body betrays me as it leans towards him, drawn like a magnet.

"Shit," James mutters under his breath before closing the distance between us. He lifts my chin with a rough hand, his thumb brushing against my flushed cheek. And then his lips crash down on mine, igniting a fire within me that burns hotter with each passing second. His arms wrap around me tightly, his touch possessive and all-consuming as he explores every inch of my body.

"James..." My mouth parts against his in a silent gasp, my voice trembling with the need for answers. "There's something I've been meaning to ask you." But he doesn't let me speak. Instead, he deepens the kiss even more, drowning out coherent thoughts or questions.

My fingers dig into James' biceps, the muscles flexing under my touch. "Please, James, we need to talk about this now." He tenses up at my touch, and his green eyes turn angrily. "I went to the garage about the the car, the one Sarah was in. The car had just been serviced. There is footage missing from the security cameras. Was it really an accident, James?"

James's expression changes as soon as the words leave my mouth, and his anger flares. "You shouldn't have gone to the garage," he growls, his voice low and dangerous. "It was reckless."

My hands land on my hips as I stare him down. "Don't act like I had any other option!" I snap, my voice dripping with frustration and anger. "I need to know the truth; she is my best friend!"

. . .

"Dammit, Ava," he mutters under his breath, raking a hand through his short hair in frustration. His eyes linger on my disheveled appearance - tousled hair, flushed cheeks, and defiant stance.

"Don't treat me like some fragile doll that needs your protection!" I push against his chest, trying to break free from his hold.

Without warning, he slams the door shut behind him with a resounding thud.

6

———————

JAMES

"What the hell were you thinking, going to the garage?" I bark, my voice a low growl.

Ava meets my gaze with equal defiance, her dark brown eyes flashing with annoyance. "I don't need your protection, James," she snaps back, her voice firm and resolute. "I can take care of myself."

That is the final straw. I can't take it anymore.

Don't you know? You are mine. Mine to protect. Mine to fuck. Mine.

I slam the door behind me and lock it in one swift motion. I turn back towards Ava, my eyes blazing. "Fine," I say, stepping forward, my eyes locked onto hers, conveying a message that needs no words.

. . .

"James..." Ava's voice barely a whisper, her breath hitching as she looks at me.

"Tell me you don't want this," I challenge, my large hands on her hips, gripping them.

"I can't," she admits, her voice barely audible.

"Good," I growl, my restraint vanishing as I crush my lips against hers. Our tongues tangled, exploring and tasting each other as if trying to quench a thirst that had been building for far too long. My hands roam over her body, feeling the softness of her curves, the heat radiating from her skin. I want all of her – every inch, every sigh, every moan that escapes her lips.

With a swift movement, I clear the desk, sending papers and the blueprint flying to the floor. I lift her onto the now-empty surface, and I position myself between her legs, our bodies pressed tightly together.

"Are you sure?" I ask, pausing for a moment to give her a chance to change her mind.

"Y-yes," Ava replies, her eyes filled with lust.

. . .

I lift her skirt and yank her panties aside, revealing her wet pussy. My fingers trace teasing circles around her clit, eliciting a gasp from her lips. The hunger in my eyes matches the fire within me, urging me to claim what is rightfully mine. I open her shirt and lower my head, capturing her hardened nipple in my mouth, suckling and nipping at it. Her back arches off the desk, pushing herself closer against me, begging for more.

I trail my kisses downwards, leaving a trail of wet heat along her abdomen until I reach the apex of her thighs. Without hesitation, I flick my tongue against her swollen clit and insert two fingers, earning a moan of pleasure that echoes through the room. I delve into her depths, tasting the sweetness that belongs solely to Ava.

The desk creaks beneath us as I devour her with a fierce hunger. Her moans grow louder, filling the room. Ava's hands grip the edge of the desk, her knuckles turning white from the force of her grip. Her body trembles beneath my touch, aching for release. I can feel her muscles tightening around my fingers, pulling me. I continue to explore every inch of her, my tongue dancing along her folds as I alternate between gentle licks and firm strokes. The taste of her arousal drives me wild. Her hips buck against my mouth, urging me for more. I oblige willingly, thrusting my fingers deeper inside her while my tongue flicks mercilessly against her sensitive clit.

"J-j-ames," Ava moans, her nails digging into my shoulders as I drive her toward the edge. "Please... don't stop."

• • •

My lips curve into a wicked smile against her heated flesh. I won't stop, not until she's unraveling in my arms, consumed by pleasure. My fingers quicken their pace, thrusting deep into her wetness while my tongue works its magic on her throbbing bud.

Ava's moans fill the room, mingling with our bodies colliding against the desk. Her back arches, her legs trembling as the intensity builds within her. I can feel her walls clenching around my fingers, desperate for release. I continue to devour her, unrelenting. The taste of her desire drives me wild.

Her cries grow louder, echoing off the walls as her climax approaches. I can sense it building within her, the tension in her body reaching its breaking point. Her back arches, her muscles tense, and with one final thrust of my fingers and flick of my tongue, she shatters, crying out my name in ecstasy.

I rise from my position between her thighs, my own desire throbbing painfully beneath my pants. I need her. Now.

In one swift motion, I discard my clothes, exposing my hardened length to the cool air of the room. Ava's eyes widen with anticipation and desire as she takes in every inch of me.

"Are you ready for me?" I ask, my voice thick with need.

. . .

"Yes," she breathes, her voice barely audible. "Please."

I grab a condom from my pocket, and I line myself up at her entrance, the head of my cock pressing against her wetness. Without breaking eye contact, I slowly plunge into her warmth, savoring the feeling of her tight walls clenching around me. Her nails dig deeper into my shoulders as she gasps, a mixture of pleasure and pain crossing her face. I hold still for a moment, allowing Ava to adjust to my size. The sensation of being buried deep inside her nearly overwhelms me. Still, I fight against it, wanting to savor every second.

With a low growl, I move, rocking my hips in a slow and deliberate rhythm. Ava's eyes flutter close, her lips parting as she moans my name. The sound ignites a fire within me, urging me to go faster and harder.

I grip her hips tightly, guiding her movements as we find our rhythm together. Each thrust pushes me closer to the edge, closer to the release I crave.

I can feel Ava's nails digging into my back as she arches against me, her body quivering in pleasure. The sound of our skin slapping together fills the room, mingling with our ragged breaths and moans.

"Harder," she gasps, her voice laced with desperation.

•   •   •

I oblige, increasing the intensity of my thrusts pounding into her. The desk shakes beneath us. Ava's legs wrap tightly around my waist, pulling me deeper inside her. Her walls pulse around me, gripping me like a vice. I can feel her release building once again. My hand slips between us, and I press my thumb against her swollen clit, rubbing in tight circles. The added stimulation pushes Ava closer to the edge. I feel her walls clenching around me, pulsing with need. But I can't let her fall over the edge just yet. Not until I've had my fill of her.

With a swift movement, I lift her off the desk and turn her around, pressing her down. She gasps in surprise, but it quickly turns into a moan as I thrust back into her from behind. The change in position allows me to penetrate even deeper, hitting all the right spots that drive her wild. Her hands reach out to grip the desk for support as I continue to pound into her relentlessly.

"Come for me, Ava," I whisper, my voice husky with desire. "Let go."Her walls clench around me, and then she comes as she cries out my name. I can't hold back any longer. With a final thrust, I find release inside her, my body shaking with the force of it. I collapse onto her, our bodies intertwined and drenched in sweat.

As she lays on the desk, I can't help but feel a surge of possessiveness and pride. I have claimed her, and she is now mine.

. . .

"Stay here," I murmur, kissing her forehead softly. "I need to check something."

Reluctantly, I peel myself away from Ava's embrace and quickly pull on my uniform. As my eyes roam around the room, they land on the blueprint scattered on the floor. My heart races as I study the detailed plans, searching for clues linking Mayor Jackson to whatever plot is unfolding in Thanksville.

And then, I see a hidden corridor behind his office leading to underground tunnels all the way to the edge of town. I trace my finger along the lines, my mind racing with possibilities. But before I can fully process this new information, my cell phone buzzes in my pocket. I retrieve it and see a text message from the Lieutenant.

My blood runs cold as I read the words - the man in the picture has been identified as a notorious hitman for the mob. Everything now seems to point towards a personal vendetta rather than a terrorist plot.

"James?" Ava calls out softly. She has just finished getting dressed. "What's going on?"

"I need access to the Mayor's office," I say bluntly.

"What do you need access to the Mayor's office for?" she asks cautiously.

. . .

"I can't explain right now."

"But...I can't," she stammers.

"Trust me," I urge, holding out my hand. Ava hesitates for a moment before nodding slowly.

7

JAMES

Ava straightens her blouse and brushes a stray strand of hair behind her ear before knocking on the heavy wooden door. "Mayor Jackson?" she calls out, her voice steady despite feeling nervous.

A clerk walking by glances at Ava before replying, "He just left the building. Seemed to be in a rush."

"Ah, I see," Ava replies casually. "I just needed some paperwork from him." The clerk shrugs and continues on his way without showing much interest.

Damn, where has he gone?

My jaw clenches and I quickly pull out my cell and fire off a text to Lieutenant Philips.

Mayor just left abruptly. Going to check the tunnel. Will update soon.

Ava fidgets with the hem of her skirt before finally mustering up the courage to push open the heavy mahogany door to Mayor Jackson's office. The click of her heels echoes through the spacious room as she enters, feeling a sense of unease wash over her.

"Stay here," I say firmly, my hand motioning for her to remain in the waiting area outside the office.

"But I—" Ava starts to protest, her lips twisting in frustration.

"Go," I command again, my tone leaving no room for argument. Reluctantly, Ava takes a step back and watches as I stride into the mayor's office. I scan the opulent room, taking in the intricate details of the dark wood paneling and the imposing presence of the large mahogany desk. My heart races as I quickly move to the bookcase lining one wall, my fingers carefully brushing against the embossed spines of leather-bound books in search of the hidden trigger that would reveal the entrance to the secret tunnel.

My breath hitches as time ticks away, my urgency growing with each passing second. Where is it?

• • •

Suddenly, my fingers brush against a small statue of a horse nestled among the books. It wobbles slightly under my touch. With a determined push, a low grinding noise fills the room as the bookcase swings outward, revealing a dark passage beyond.

Gotcha! I whisper triumphantly. I open the hidden tunnel and I see Ava fidgeting in the doorway, her bottom lip caught between her teeth. My heart tightens with worry for her safety.

"Listen," I say, my voice firm and commanding. "I need you to stay out here. If anything happens, call for backup immediately. Do you understand?" She hesitates but nods in agreement.

"Please be careful," she whispers, her voice trembling.

"Always am," I reply reassuringly, trying to ease her worries. I prop a heavy bronze paperweight against the rotating bookcase to keep it from closing and trapping me inside. As I step into the dark, narrow tunnel, my senses go on high alert. The musty smell of damp walls and the sound of water trickling echoes in the distance. My skin prickles with unease as I cautiously make my way.

"Dammit, Ava!" I hiss, spotting her crouched near the entrance. "I told you to stay put." But before I can scold her further, she stumbles forward, her foot catching on something hidden in the darkness. In a panic, she reaches out and accidentally pushes against the rotating bookcase. A heavy bronze paperweight falls to the ground with a loud thud, causing the secret door to slam shut behind us.

"Shit!" I curse under my breath, "We are trapped."

"James, I'm so sorry," Ava whispers, her voice trembling as she fights back tears. "I didn't mean to—"

"It's okay," *baby, don't cry.* "We need to find the way out of here."

Ava nods, her eyes wide with fear. I examine the blueprint, tracing every twist and turn of the tunnel with my finger.

"Stick close to me and don't touch anything," I order.

With my flashlight, I lead us deeper into the dark depths, searching for the way out. The walls are slick with moisture, and the floor is uneven under our feet. Ava's breathing becomes rapid and shallow, her chest heaving with each step. Our footsteps echo loudly off the damp walls as we navigate the narrow passageway.

"Stay right behind me," I command in a low voice, my body tense. As a highly-trained SEAL, I know how to handle dangerous situations like this, but all that matters to me now is keeping Ava safe.

. . .

As we round a sharp bend in the dark tunnel, my flashlight illuminates a small alcove in the wall. My heart lurches as I spot an ominous-looking device nestled within – a crude, homemade explosive wired to a digital timer.

"Shit," I mutter, my grip on the flashlight tightening. "Ava, stay back. I need to get a closer look at this thing."

Ava's face pales as she glances at the bomb and then back at me. "What is it?"

"It's an explosive," I answer tersely, my eyes never leaving the device. "You need to start retracing our steps and walk back as far as possible."

Panic rising in her voice, Ava presses further. "What kind of explosive?"

"I don't know yet," I admit.

"I am not going anywhere without you."

I can't argue right now. I kneel beside it, my fingers flying over the tangled wires and connections, trying to figure out if I can disarm it.

· · ·

"Do you know what you're doing?" Her voice quivers with fear.

"Please, just give me space," I reply, my mind racing as time ticks away. My gaze flicks between the blueprint of the tunnel and the bomb in front of me. Every detail is crucial if we want to make it out alive. With a grunt, I hoist the explosive into my arms, cradling it like a fragile baby.

"Go back," I plead. She is not moving. "Fine," I mutter.

I move quickly through the dimly lit tunnel, the heavy weight of the explosive in my arms. Sweat drips down my brow, and my muscles aching from the strain. As I reach a fork in the tunnel, I hesitate for a split second, consulting the mental map I have created. There is no room for error.

Just a few more feet, I push my body to its limits as I race down the corridor.

At last, I reach the opening. With mere seconds to spare, I hurl the explosive through the open hatch, praying it would be enough to shield us from the blast.

"Get down!" I shout. The deafening blast tears through the air as the device detonates in a cloud of dust and debris; I grab Ava and pull her to the ground, shielding her with my body, taking the brunt of the impact. As the dust settles, I can feel the warm stickiness of blood.

"James down!" I hear shouting through the haze. "Get him out of here, now!"

I hear Mike and Tyler, their boots crunching on shattered glass and twisted metal. "Stay with us, Jim," one urges. "We're gonna get you fixed up."

The world seems to fade in and out.

"Where's... Ava?" I gasp, my thoughts racing back to the woman who had captured my heart like no other.

"Safe," comes the terse reply from one of my brothers-in-arms. "You did good, man."

"Move it, guys!" the Lieutenant barks. "I want Jim in surgery yesterday!"

"Safe." I cling to that single word. And then everything goes dark.

EPILOGUE

AVA

I grip James's hand tightly, the calloused skin rough against my softer palm. The hospital bed creaks under his weight as he lies still, his body covered in bruises and cuts.

The heart monitor beeps steadily in the background, a constant reminder of the fragile state James is in. I trace the veins on his bruised hand with my finger, trying to hold back the tears that threaten to fall.

"James," I whisper, my voice cracking with emotion. "Please wake up. I need you."

His fingers twitch within mine, and his eyelids flutter open slowly. His intense green gaze meets mine, and for a moment, everything else fades away.

"Hey beautiful," he rasps, managing a weak smile.

. . .

My heart might burst as I reply, "James, you're awake."

"Wouldn't want to miss anything," he jokes weakly. "Especially not when you're around."

I sniffle and bury my face in his chest. "Thank you," I manage to say between sobs.

He pulls me closer, cradling my head against his shoulder. His thumb gently wipes away my tears as he whispers sweet words of comfort. "Baby," he begins, his voice filled with emotion.

"You don't have to say anything now; just rest."I stop him and shake my head, pulling back to look at him.

"Shh," he silences me with a soft kiss on my forehead. "Ava, I love you more than anything in this world. You are my obsession, my saving grace, so I keep fighting."

My heart clenches.

"Promise me," he continues, his voice barely audible. "Promise me you'll never doubt how much you mean to me."

. . .

I nod without hesitation. "I promise."

His body sinks into the mattress, a deep exhale escaping his lips. "I'm not going anywhere," he says, his eyes softening as they meet mine. "You're stuck with me, beautiful."

A playful glint flashes in his eyes as I reply, "Stuck with you? Hmm, I don't know if I can handle that."

"Too late," he grins, pulling me closer and planting a sweet kiss on my lips. "Forever, Ava," he whispers against my lips, warmth spreading through my body at the words. "You and me, forever."

SEALED PURSUIT

A SPICY OTT INSTALOVE ROMANCE

1

LISA

Thanksville is preparing to commemorate Captain Armstrong: the town is adorned with banners bearing his face and the words "Forever Our Hero." Even the local children have joined in on the tribute, their hand-drawn posters taped to storefront windows. At the heart of it all stands a magnificent bronze statue, a constant reminder of the man who gave his life for freedom.

As I make my way to the town square, notebook and pen in hand, I feel heaviness settle over me. This is not my first time covering the anniversary celebrations of Captain Armstrong's death in battle. Every year, the town comes together to honor its fallen hero, and every year, it feels like a repetitive ordeal that drags on forever.

"Lisa, don't forget to interview some of the townspeople," my editor's voice echoes as I scan the area for potential subjects. "We want to capture the true spirit of this event."

. . .

"Of course," I replied through gritted teeth, hiding my true feelings.

"Great," he smiled, oblivious to my disappointment. "This is an important event for our community."

I sigh as I glance around at the banners and posters plastered everywhere, each more patriotic than the last. It's not that I don't respect Captain Armstrong's sacrifice – far from it. But after covering the same story year after year, I can't help but long for something more exciting.

As I go through the sea of red, white, and blue decorations, an old lady stops me with a trembling hand on my arm. "Excuse me, Miss Timpin?" she says excitedly. "Would you like to interview me about my memories of the Captain ? I knew him personally, you know."

"Of course," I smile and pull out my notebook as she speaks, jotting down her words. But in my mind, all I can think about is the big story I could be working on instead. A scandal, a mystery - anything but this annual fluff piece.

"Thank you," I say mechanically when she finishes, forcing myself to look interested. "Your memories of Captain Armstrong will greatly add to our tribute."

There must be something more to this story, I tell myself. *If only I could find the hidden angle that would turn this piece into a grip-ping, front-page-worthy investigation.*

As I walk away, my eyes scan the venue for the charity ball I'm covering for the paper.

I hope Jessica has some interesting information or angle …

As I enter the facility, a burly man in a red baseball cap shouts, "Alright, let's get this stage set up!" His voice breaks me from my thoughts as I watch a team of workers scurry around, hoisting wooden beams and hammering nails with precision.

A familiar voice calls out my name – Jessica who is in charge of the events committee this year. "Can you believe it's been twenty-five years already?" she exclaims excitedly.

"Time flies," I reply with a forced smile. Inside, I can't help but wonder how many more anniversaries like this I'll have to cover before finally getting a real story.

"Are you okay?" Jessica asks, her brow furrowing in concern. "You seem...distracted."

"Just thinking," I admit, my eyes drifting back to the construction of the stage. The crew is now hoisting a massive banner above it, their muscles straining with effort.

. . .

"Thinking about what?" Jessica presses, her curiosity piqued. "About how this story could be so much more than just another tribute," I confess quietly. "About how there must be something hidden beneath the surface – some secret waiting to be uncovered." My gaze lingers on the crew as they continue their work.

Jessica's gentle touch on my arm pulls me out of my thoughts, and I turn to face her. "Lisa, sometimes a story is just a story," she says, her voice soothing like a lullaby. "Not everything has to be a scandal or a mystery."

I nod absently, my gaze lingering on the stage before us as the final decorations are placed. The faint chatter fills the air, but I am drawn to a figure striding confidently through the crowd. He stands out amongst the vibrant celebration preparations, tall and muscular with an air of authority that seems out of place.

"Who's that?" I ask Jessica, nodding towards the man as he approaches the stage.

"That's Tyler Johnson," she replies. "He's one of the Navy SEALs here to help with the celebrations." It's not unusual to see military personnel around town during these events.

My curiosity piques, and I watch Tyler survey the stage with a critical eye. Something about him draws me in, and I can't help but feel a spark of attraction.

"Lisa Timpin," I introduce myself, extending my hand to him. "Thanksville Gazette."

"Tyler Johnson," he replies, firmly shaking my hand before those piercing blue eyes lock onto mine. "Nice to meet you."

Despite trying to maintain my composure, I can feel the heat rising in my cheeks at his intense gaze. Maybe this year's tribute won't be so dull after all.

"Are you enjoying your time in Thanksville, Tyler?" I ask, hoping for any information. My investigative journalist instincts kick in.

Tyler's guarded expression softens as I speak, and I can tell he is trying to choose his words carefully."It's a nice town," he replies, glancing around. "The people here have been very welcoming."

"Have you been involved in the preparations for Captain Armstrong's anniversary celebration?" I prod, watching his reaction closely.

"I've been lending a hand where I can," he admits with a small smile, his eyes drifting back to the stage where preparations were underway.

Just as I was about to ask him more questions, "Lisa," Jessica calls me away.

"Right," I say, smiling as I turn back to Tyler. "Well, enjoy the rest of your stay, and maybe I'll see you around."

"Thank you," he nods politely, his eyes lingering on mine for a moment longer than necessary. He's unlike anyone I've ever encountered – mysterious, handsome, and undeniably alluring.

"Well, if you ever need a local's perspective or someone to show you around, I'm your girl," I add, just in case.

"Sounds like a plan," he agrees, his gaze locked on mine, a spark igniting between us. As Tyler walks away from me, I can't help but notice the strong curve of his back beneath his uniform.

"Lisa!" Jessica calls out, snapping me back to reality. "Are you even listening?"

"Sorry," I mutter, snapping back to reality. Jessica arches a perfectly sculpted eyebrow at me, clearly amused by my distracted state. "My mind was just...elsewhere."

. . .

"Clearly," She leans in, her eyes twinkling with mischief. "Thinking about Tyler, huh? You've got it bad."

"Maybe just a little," heat rises to my cheeks as I try to play it cool, but deep down, I know she's right. It's more than just a crush; something about this mysterious SEAL draws me in, awakening my dormant reporter instincts.

Jessica checks her watch and sighs. "I have a meeting in five minutes. You'll be okay here?" I nod, waving her off as she hurries off.

Workers, dressed in dusty overalls and hefting heavy tools, meticulously construct the stage for the charity ball. The thud of hammers and the clank of metal against metal fills the air.

"Look out!" someone shouts suddenly just as a section of the scaffolding comes crashing down, sending a dust cloud billowing into the air.

"Is everyone okay?" My heart races as I rush over to assist, my mind buzzing with questions.

"Thankfully, no one was hurt," a worker replies, his voice shaky but grateful. Something about this incident doesn't sit right with me, and I can't shake the feeling that there's more to the story than meets the eye.

. . .

A group of Navy SEALs stands to the side, going through the debris with guarded expressions. Suddenly, their boss rushes in. He is standing in the middle of the ballroom surveying the area when suddenly he turns back, his eyes fixed firmly on Jessica, who is peeking through the door.

"I told you not to move," he tells her.

"I know, but ..." she replies sheepishly.

"No, but," he cuts her off sharply. "... go back home ... Now". His voice is very stern. Jessica quickly turns away and goes as if hypnotized.

What is going on?

I take a deep breath before approaching the construction workers. "Hey," I say casually, trying to keep my tone light despite my rising agitation. "Can you guys help me out? I'm writing an article on the event, and I want to make sure everything is covered for safety purposes."

The workers exchange wary glances before one finally responds. "It was just an accident. These things happen," he says quickly, avoiding my gaze and signaling the end of the conversation.

. . .

My determination only grows stronger in the face of their resistance."I understand that, but can you tell me more about what happened? Was there any negligence or equipment failure?" The workers seem hesitant to speak, but I refuse to back down. Finally, I approach one, cleaning up the debris from the collapse. "Excuse me," I begin, "do you have any idea what caused this?"

"Uh, not really sure, ma'am," he mutters, wiping the sweat off his brow with the back of his hand.

"Come on, there must be something," I press, frustrated.

"Look, lady, it was just an accident, okay?" he snaps, and I can see he won't give me anything else.

I sigh, my eyes scanning the area for clues that might lead me in the right direction. Something isn't adding up, and I'm determined to find out what it is.

Think, Lisa, my mind racing with possibilities. Could the collapse simply be an accident, or is there more to it than meets the eye?

I grab my purse and pull out a small notebook, scribbling down my questions. Could Tyler know something about the incident? And how can I get him to open up to me if he does?

• • •

Get close to him, I scribble in my notebook, feeling excited and nervous at the thought of getting closer to Tyler for both professional and personal reasons.

Fine, I say as I hit the road. *Let's do this, Lisa.*

The next few hours are a whirlwind, searching for clues all over town. But as much as I try, I can't find anything concrete.

Ugh, I groan, slamming my fist on the steering wheel in frustration. *What am I missing?*

My phone buzzes in my purse, and I fish it out to see a text from Tyler.

> Hey, I'm free tonight if you want to grab a drink

I feel a flutter at the thought of spending an evening with him.

> Perfect

My mind already racing with ideas on subtly questioning him about the incident.

. . .

Sounds like a date

He texts back, and I can't help but smile, despite my growing unease .

As I sit in front of my vanity mirror, carefully applying a bold shade of red lipstick and adjusting my dress, I can't help but feel torn between my professional instincts and the undeniable attraction I have for Tyler. But I know I'm onto something big, and I won't let my feelings get in the way of exposing the truth.

Alright, I say to my reflection, steeling myself for the night ahead. *Let's find out what's happening in this town.*

2

TYLER

As I stand amidst the chaos and commotion, my boots crunch against the debris from the collapsed scaffolding. My lungs fill with the acrid scent of dust and sweat as workers frantically clear the mess.

Shit, I curse. *This wasn't part of the plan.*

I scan the crowd with narrowed eyes, searching for signs of danger or sabotage. But then I see her - a woman with dark hair, piercing green eyes, and curves that make my pulse race. Lisa. She's still here, her curiosity piqued by the incident. I feel a wave of irritation and attraction wash over me as I watch her step closer to the scene, her brow furrowed in concentration. I have to resist the urge to run over and pull her away from it all.

As I watch Lisa weave through the small crowd, my heart

races. I know I have a job to do, but all I can think about is how much I want her.

Stay focused, Tyler, I remind myself again. *You can't let distractions get in the way.*

Lisa marches towards the group of workers, her eyes intensifying with determination. She whips out a leather-bound notebook and clicks her pen, ready to jot down every detail. I study the way her hips sway with each confident step, the curve of her waist, and the swell of her chest beneath that blouse that clings to her figure.

"Can you tell me what happened here?" she asks a worker, her voice authoritative yet gentle. The worker hesitates for a moment before explaining how the scaffolding seemed to just give way without warning.

"Was anyone up there when it collapsed?" she inquires, scribbling notes as she moves from one person to another, piecing together the story like a puzzle.

"No, thankfully," someone replies, and I breathe a sigh of relief.

Something doesn't feel right. It's almost too convenient that no one was hurt. The team scatters, searching for any clues and talking to the workers about anything suspicious they might have seen.

· · ·

"Did anyone see anything out of the ordinary before it fell?" I hear Lisa ask another witness, her voice closer now. I can smell her perfume – a mix of jasmine and something citrusy – and it sends a shiver down my spine.

Stay focused, I remind myself, gritting my teeth.

"Tyler, there's something you need to see," one of my teammates calls out, beckoning me over. I glance back at Lisa.

"Tell me you've found something," I say, tense and impatient.

"We have," he replies. "But it's not good."

As we piece together the evidence, I feel a growing dread - this wasn't an accident.

The moment Lieutenant Jake Philips bursts into the room, I can feel the urgency in his stride. "Report!" he barks, and my teammates quickly fill him in on the sabotaged scaffolding.

"Keep this under wraps," Philips orders. "We don't need any panic." He scans the area, his eyes stopping abruptly when they land on Lisa. She's still asking questions, her brow furrowed in determination as she listens intently to a worker's story.

. . .

"Who is she?" Jake demands, pointing at her.

"Lisa," I answer, keeping my voice steady. "Local reporter."

"Get her out of here," he says, shooting me a pointed glare.

I swallow the lump in my throat as I watch her. Her dark hair falls gently over her shoulders, framing her face as she jots down notes.

"Lisa," I call out, trying to keep my tone casual as I approach her. She looks up, her green eyes shining with curiosity.

"Tyler," she greets, flashing me a smile that sends my heart racing. "Did you find anything?"

"Actually," I begin hesitantly, "I think it's time for you to leave."

"Excuse me?" she asks, her eyebrows raised in surprise.

"Look, it's not safe here right now," I insist, glancing nervously back at Philips, who's watching us closely.

. . .

"Are you kidding?" she retorts, anger flaring in her eyes. "There's a story here, Tyler. A big one. And I'm not leaving until I get to the bottom of it."

"Lisa, this is non-negotiable," I say firmly, trying to ignore how her chest rises and falls with each breath.

"Fine." She crosses her arms, her expression defiant. "But you better believe I won't stop digging until I find out what happened here."

"Understood," I reply, my jaw clenched as I watch her walk away. I can feel the Lieutenant's eyes on me, his disapproval palpable.

"Handle her, Tyler," he orders, and I nod.

"Got it, sir," I say, trying to push aside the growing desire that threatens to consume me. There is nothing more I want than to handle every single bit of her. This mission just got a whole lot more complicated.

I watch as Lisa's hips sway when she walks away from me, her form-fitting jeans accentuating the curve of her thighs. My frustration and desire for her grow in equal measure. I know this is a dangerous combination, but it's impossible to ignore.

. . .

"Tyler!" Lieutenant Philips snaps, pulling me back to reality. "You need to handle this situation."

"Sir, I'll make sure she stays out of our way," I promise, my voice betraying a hint of reluctance.

"Good." He nods curtly, his eyes still fixed on Lisa, who's been escorted out.

Damn it, I need to keep her at arm's length, but I can't get her out of my head. Every time I close my eyes, I see her, those green eyes burning into me, and the way her body moves, curving like a siren song.

Focus, Tyler, I mutter under my breath, my fingers tapping against the steering wheel as I drive through the small town.

My phone buzzes, startling me. It's a text from Lieutenant Philips:

Any progress with Lisa?

As if on cue, I spot her walking down the sidewalk, her long legs carrying her gracefully. I pull over, watching her for a moment before making my decision.

• • •

Here goes nothing, I sigh, grabbing my phone and quickly jotting down a message to Lisa.

> Hey, it's Tyler. How about we grab a drink tonight? I promise, no work talk.

I hit send before I can second-guess myself, my pulse racing in anticipation. What am I doing?

A moment later, her response comes through:

> Sure, why not? Let's meet at The Rusty Anchor at 8.

> Great, see you there

I reply.

The Rusty Anchor is dimly lit, the soft murmur of conversation creating a cozy atmosphere. I fidget in my seat, awaiting Lisa's arrival. I can't help but wonder what she's wearing and how she'll look when she walks in.

"Tyler?" Her voice cuts through my thoughts like a knife, sending tingles down my spine.

. . .

"Lisa." I turn to face her, immediately struck by how stunning she looks. Her dress clings to every delicious curve, and her hair cascades down her back like a silk waterfall.

"Hi." A playful smile dances across her lips, causing my heart to race. "Thanks for inviting me out."

"Anytime," I manage to reply, unable to take my eyes off her. "I thought we could both use a break."

She slides onto the barstool beside me, her long legs clad in black tights and ankle boots.

"What are you drinking?" she asks, flashing a bright smile.

"Whiskey on the rocks," I respond, signaling the bartender to pour another glass.

As our fingers brush while reaching for our drinks, a surge of electricity courses through my body down to my cock. Trying to compose myself, I take a deep breath and meet her gaze. She's even more beautiful up close.

Her whiskey glass clinks against the table. "Do you really believe it was an accident?" she questions, her tone betraying her skepticism. "Come on," she presses. "You were there, and you're a SEAL. You must have some idea of what happened."

She's relentless in her pursuit of the truth, and as much as it drives me crazy, it turns me on.

Damn it, why does she have to be so hot?

Every fiber of my being wants to lean in and kiss her, but I hold back, not wanting to ruin the moment. But as she looks at me with those mesmerizing green eyes, I know it's only a matter of time before I give in. I interlace my fingers with hers, hoping to calm her down. "Let's not talk about work tonight," I say softly.

She reluctantly takes a sip of her drink before sighing. But I can see the gears turning in her head; she won't let this go quickly.

"Tell me about yourself," I suggest, changing the subject. "What brought you to journalism?"

As she speaks, her eyes sparkle with nostalgia for her college days. She gestures animatedly with her hands as she recounts her first big story and how she developed a passion for chasing the truth. But as we sit in the crowded bar, I can't help but notice her glancing around nervously.

Suddenly, she leans in closer and lowers her voice. "Tyler," she says. "I overheard some people talking earlier. They mentioned something about the scaffolding being sabotaged. Do you think–"

. . .

"Lisa," I interrupt, my heart racing. "Tonight is not about work."

She sighs and looks down at her drink, fidgeting with the straw. "Sorry," she mumbles. "I just can't shake off this feeling of unease. This whole situation has me on edge."

"We can't let it distract us from our other task," I say gently.

"Like what?" she asks, raising an eyebrow.

"Like this," I reply, unable to resist any longer. I lean in and press my lips against hers. The kiss is electric, sending shivers down my spine. Her juicy red lips are soft and warm, and she tastes like whiskey and desire. I know I shouldn't be doing this – it's dangerous, reckless – but I don't care. All that matters is Lisa and the feel of her against me. I pull away slowly, our breaths mingling in the air between us. Her eyes are wide and filled with surprise.

"Tyler," she whispers, her voice heavy with need. "What was that?"

"It's something I've wanted to do since the moment I laid eyes on you," I admit, my heart still pounding. This is a mistake, but it's a mistake I'm willing to make.

. . .

"Maybe we should focus on that for now," she suggests seductively.

3

LISA

My desk is cluttered with files and scribbled notes, the chaos on its way to swallowing me whole. As I sit there, my heart races as I replay last night's kiss. Tyler's lips were tender and insistent, igniting a fire within me that still hasn't died down. I force myself to focus on work.

Damn it, Lisa, under my breath. It's hard, though, when all I want is to relive that moment again and again.

My fingers graze over a file, but my thoughts drift back to how Tyler walked me home afterwards. He was a true gentleman, not pushing for anything more, even though we both wanted it. And oh, how badly I wanted him—all of him—but he held back, making my heart race in ways I never thought possible.

"Lisa?" a colleague calls out, interrupting my daydream.

•   •   •

I startle, feeling embarrassed by my own thoughts. "Uh, yeah?" I reply.

"You seem...distracted," the voice says with a hint of amusement.

"Just...thinking about some things," I admit, feeling the heat rise in my cheeks. "Nothing important."

"Alright then," the voice responds before fading away, leaving me to my thoughts again. I shake my head, trying to remove distractions and force myself to focus on the task. There's work to be done, and I can't afford to let my personal life interfere. But deep down, as much as I try to focus on the files, the notes, and the investigation, I yearn for his touch, smile, and kisses.

Get a grip, Lisa, I chastise myself. *Control,* clenching my jaw and forcing myself to push away from my desk.

I walk to the window and stare out at the lights outside. I take a deep breath and reach for the phone, my hand trembling as I dial the number. The ringing line echoes through the quiet office, mingling with the rush of thoughts in my mind. Images of Tyler's lips on mine flood my mind, and I shake my head to clear them away.

A gruff voice answers, jolting me back to reality. "Hello?"

• • •

My heart races as I introduce myself as Lisa from the Thanksville Gazette and explain my reason for calling - investigating the scaffolding collapse from yesterday.

"Was your company involved in the cleanup or reconstruction?" I ask, forcing myself to stay on track.

"Sorry, lady," the man replies after a brief pause. "We weren't called in for that job. Can't help you." Disappointment settles in my chest as I thank him and hang up the phone. Another dead end. I scribble a note on my pad, crossing off the construction company from my list of potential leads for the story. I'll have to keep digging.

As I sit at my desk, the image of Jessica being bossed around by the boss SEAL keeps replaying in my mind. It doesn't sit right with me. I tried to call her last night after my date with Tyler, but she didn't pick up. I check my phone for missed calls. None. I redial her number, desperate to make sure she's okay.

"Where are you, Jess?" I whisper under my breath. The phone rings several times before she answers, sounding exhausted and elated simultaneously. A wave of relief washes over me, but my concern remains.

"I was so worried about you. Are you okay? What happened with the Lieutenant SEAL yesterday?" I ask.

· · ·

"Lisa, I'm fine," she insists, though her words don't convince me entirely. "Don't worry."

"What about the ball? Is everything going to be okay?" I ask, thinking about the stage.

"Oh, Jake took care of it," she replies with a tired yet cheerful voice. "He had his team and some people from the nearby Navy base come in to fix the scaffolding. It's all back to normal now."

I pause for a moment, choosing my words carefully. "Why didn't he just hire a local company? It seems odd that he'd use his own team and military personnel."

Jessica shrugs nonchalantly. "Jake wanted to ensure everything goes smoothly for the charity ball. He thought it would be more efficient to use the resources he already has available."

"Efficient or controlling?" I raise an eyebrow skeptically.

"Lisa, don't start," Jessica sighs, annoyance creeping into her tone. "Jake just wants this event to be a success. Let's not turn this into some kind of conspiracy."

"Alright, alright," I reluctantly acquiesce, sensing her growing frustration. "I just find it odd, that's all."

. . .

"Trust me, there's nothing to worry about," she insists. "Now, can we please talk about something else? Like how excited I am ?"

"Okay, okay, I'm sorry," I say, forcing myself to switch gears. Inside, though, the nagging feeling of suspicion remains.

"Good," she says, her tone lightening. "Now, let's focus on having a fantastic time at the ball!"

I try to force myself to join in her excitement, but a small voice in my mind nags at me. There's something off about this whole situation. "Alright, sounds like a plan," I finally agree, though my heart isn't entirely in it. I hang up the phone and take a deep breath. But as I turn back to my desk and the list of leads in front of me, I can't ignore the lingering anticipation of seeing Tyler again.

Focus, Lisa, I remind myself sternly. *This is not about Tyler; it's about finding the truth*, but the image of his handsome face and muscular arms refuses to leave my mind.

———

I stare at my reflection in the full-length mirror, examining every inch of the sleek black gown hugging my curves. The silky fabric feels cool against my skin, but I can't seem to shake off the chill in the pit of my stomach. My conversation with Jessica plays on repeat in my mind as I carefully apply a bold swipe of red lipstick.

Her words were laced with tension when she mentioned Jake, and her defensiveness only fuels my curiosity. I wonder if something is going on between them. But no, I push the thought away. Maybe they are just friends, and I'm over-thinking things. But then, why did she seem so secretive? And why was she so quick to dismiss my concerns?

Stop it, I scold myself, shaking my head to clear my thoughts. Tonight is about the charity ball. A flutter of excitement courses through me at the thought of seeing Tyler again after our unforgettable kiss last night.

I carefully gather my long, dark hair and twist it into an intricate bun, securing it with bobby pins that glint in the light. My ears are adorned with chandelier earrings and a matching necklace that sparkles like diamonds against my skin. As I take a deep breath, trying to push aside the nagging doubts that plague me, the sound of crinkling satin fills the room.

Alright, Lisa, you've got this, giving one last glance at my reflection before grabbing a sleek clutch and heading out the door.

When I enter the grand ballroom, the air is alive with chatter and music. Ladies twirl in vibrant dresses while gentlemen stand tall in sharp tuxedos. Despite the hustle and bustle, I quickly find Jessica and Jake standing off the side.

Jake's hands are clenched tightly at his sides, and his jaw is determined. At the same time, Jessica's eyes dart back and forth between him and another SEAL who stands nearby. It's clear they're having a serious conversation; from the looks of it, there may be more between them than just friendship.

"Lisa!" Tyler's familiar voice breaks through my thoughts, and I turn to see him approaching me in his crisp dress uniform. "You look absolutely stunning."

I turn to face him, "Thank you," I say, trying to keep my voice steady as I tear my gaze away from Jess and Jake.

God, he looks so handsome.

"Shall we dance?" he asks, extending his arm towards me. Without hesitation, I take it and let him lead me to the center of the dance floor. As we move in sync with the music, his intense gaze, filled with unmistakable desire, never leaves mine. In this moment, nothing else matters - just us. We belong to each other, and that's all that counts.

4

TYLER

I can't stop thinking about her. Lisa. The way her lips felt against mine, the softness of her skin as my hands ran down her back. I wanted to claim her then and there, but duty called, and I had to return to the venue.

"Tyler, focus," Mike's voice breaks through my thoughts. "We need to finish up here."

"Yeah, yeah," I say, refocusing. We've been working all night to rebuild the stage. It's clear that it wasn't an accident – someone sabotaged it. And we have to ensure no more surprises are waiting for us.

"Hey, man, you okay?" Mike's concern was evident in his eyes. He's known me long enough to recognize when something's off.

· · ·

"I'm fine," I grumble, determined not to let my thoughts of Lisa jeopardize our mission. But as we sweep the building for explosives, all I can think about is holding her again and claiming her as mine.

"Alright, guys," our lieutenant announces as we finish. "Everything looks good. Let's get some rest before the event starts. Take turns keeping watch."

"Copy that," I reply, my voice steady despite the turmoil inside me.

I make my rounds as the guests arrive, ensuring everything runs smoothly. The lively beat of music fills the air, and drinks are poured left and right. Smiling faces and relaxed chatter confirm that everyone is having a good time. The Mayor will be here soon for the speech.

Suddenly, a delivery truck catches my eye as it pulls into the parking lot. "Mike, something's off with that truck," I say, gesturing towards the vehicle.

"I'll go check it out," he replies, scanning through his clipboard for anything about a scheduled delivery. Everything seems to be in order except for one thing – there is no mention of a cake.

"Mike, Tyler, keep an eye on things inside and make sure nothing goes wrong with the Mayor." The lieutenant instructs and gathers Derek and the others to investigate, leaving Mike and me on watch.

I can't afford to be distracted right now, but that's easier said than done when I spot her across the room. Lisa, a vision in a plunging black dress, takes my breath away. My body responds instantly, my cock hard as hell.

"Hey, Lisa," I managed to say through gritted teeth, fighting the urge to pull her into my arms and never let go. "You look beautiful." She should be mine, only mine.

"Tyler! You're here!" Her surprise quickly turns into a warm smile.

"Care for a dance?" I ask, extending my hand towards her.

"Of course." she nods, her hand sliding into mine. The contact sends a jolt of electricity up my arm and down my cock. As we sway to the music, I struggle to keep my composure and not draw her closer. Her soft breath tickles my neck, and I can feel the heat radiating from her body.

"Tyler," she murmurs, her voice barely above a whisper. "What happened last night? Why did you leave so suddenly?"

"Duty call," I growl, trying to will myself to stay focused on our surroundings instead of how she feels against me.

. . .

"Okay," she concedes, her eyes searching mine for answers. But my priority right now is keeping her safe – far from whatever danger lurked outside these walls. As the song ends, I reluctantly release her from my embrace.

"Tyler," Mike whispers, nudging me back to reality. "We need to start mingling."

I nod, trying to control the urge to ravage her right there and then. My eyes dart around the crowded room, scanning for any potential threats. I can feel my muscles tensing as I force myself to stay alert. But every time I steal a glance at her, my mind goes wild with desire – it takes all my willpower not to pounce on her. My cock is so hard it hurts.

Lisa's infectious laugh echoes through the room, drawing me in like a magnet. She moves gracefully through the crowd, her hips swaying to the music with a mesmerizing rhythm.

"Excuse me," she says in a soft, melodic voice that sends shivers down my spine. I see her standing near the exit, curiosity gleaming in her eyes as she watches our team gather outside. My instincts kick in, and I know I must intercept her before she gets too curious for her own good.

"Lisa," I call out, striding towards her. She looks at me with confusion etched on her features, but I don't give her a chance to speak. My arms wrap around her waist, and I pull her close, capturing her lips in a searing kiss.

"Tyler," she gasps when I reluctantly break the kiss, her cheeks flushed with desire. "What was that for?"

"I couldn't resist any longer," I confess huskily.

"Tyler," the lieutenant's voice crackles through my radio. "All clear."

Lisa's eyes sparkle, her curiosity piqued. Still, before she can ask any questions, I silence her with another passionate kiss. My hands roam over her body, memorizing every curve and dip as if they were made for me.

This woman is mine, and I'll do whatever it takes to possess her, to protect . No one will ever hurt her – not while I'm alive.

5

LISA

The cool night air whispers against my bare arms, and my heels click loudly on the pavement as I make my way to the car. My mind is in a frenzy, replaying the voice, "All clear." Clear of what? What danger were they clearing out?

As I approach the edge of the parking lot, I see a group of SEALs huddled behind the building. Tyler stands apart from them, his muscular frame silhouetted against the darkness. My heart flutters at the sight of him, and memories of our steamy kiss flood my mind.

I can't stop thinking about his strong arms around me as we kissed, his breath warm against my neck. My skin tingles at the memory. I'm soaking wet and need to change out of this dress.

. . .

At home, I peel off the clingy fabric and quickly shower. The hot shower does little to calm the fire that Tyler ignited within me. Every inch of my body craves his touch. As I collapse into bed, I can't stop thinking about his touch, scent, and taste.

A sudden tap on my bedroom window startles me awake. I rush to open it, and Tyler is there, looking up at me intensely. I hurry down to let him in, pulse racing. He shuts the door behind us with a swift kick and presses me against it, his hands exploring every curve of my body. Thoughts vanish, replaced by pure desire. Tonight, I am his, and he is mine. I melt into him, my hands roaming over his muscular back as our kiss deepens.

"Bedroom," he growls against my lips.

"Down the hall, on the right." My voice comes out breathy.

His muscles flex as he lifts me effortlessly into his arms and carries me to the bed. His rough, calloused hands explore every inch of my bare skin, sending sparks of electricity through me. I tug at his jacket, desperate to feel more of him against me. He swiftly removes it, revealing a chiseled chest I can't resist running my hands over.

He hovers above me, his hunger and need evident in the way he devours my lips with his own. I arch my back, craving more of his touch, as his strong fingers find their way to my breasts and squeeze them.

. . .

I gasp and moan as he moves down my body, leaving a trail of fire with each kiss. My nails dig into his back, urging him on. He positions himself between my legs and locks eyes with me. We both know what will happen, and the anticipation is almost unbearable.

Tyler's warm breath tickles my inner thigh, creating a tingling sensation that spreads through my body. My fingers tangle in his hair, pulling him closer, urging him to continue. The soft graze of his lips against my sensitive skin drives me wild with anticipation.

Then, with a deliberate slowness that tortures me most exquisitely, Tyler's tongue finally makes contact. A moan escapes my lips as a surge of pleasure courses through my body. Every stroke of his skilled tongue sends waves of pleasure coursing through me, making it impossible for me to stay still. My back arches off the bed as my hands clutch at the sheets beneath me.

His fingers dig into my thighs, holding me in place as he continues to tease and tantalize me with his mouth. The intensity builds as he flicks and sucks, driving me wild with need. I moan uncontrollably, unable to contain the pleasure that is consuming me.

I feel myself reaching the peak, my body coiled tightly like a spring ready to release. Tyler senses it, too, and increases his pace, pushing me closer and closer to the edge. I can feel his own need growing, his arousal pressing against my thigh. It only fuels my desire further, pushing me closer to the edge.

And then it happens. My vision blurs as I cry out his name, lost in the pleasure of the moment. Tyler doesn't stop there; he sheds the last remnants of clothing and positions himself between my legs, his length pressing against my entrance. A low, guttural growl escapes his throat as he pushes himself inside me, filling me completely.

In a moment of clarity, I remember the condom and say, "Condom...side table."

He pulls out slowly, rummaging through the drawer for a condom while I wait with bated breath. When he rolls it on, our eyes lock in a heated gaze before he plunges back inside me.

The sensation of him stretching me, filling me, sends waves of pleasure throughout my body. I cling to him, my nails digging into his back as I urge him deeper. With each thrust, Tyler's pace quickens, and our bodies move together in perfect rhythm.

Then suddenly, he stops and slooowly pulls out.

My body protests at the loss of contact. "N-no, please, fuck me, "I whimper in need of more. He withdraws from me entirely and spins me around, pushing me towards the edge of the bed.

"You want me to fuck you hard, don't you?"

"Y-yes," I scream.

My heart races with anticipation as I brace myself with my hands on the mattress. Tyler's strong hands grip my hips tightly as he enters me from behind, his thrusts deep, forceful, and unrelenting. His fingers trail over my body, exploring every curve and crevice. Suddenly, he pulls out again, gripping my butt cheeks and spreading them apart to reveal my tight opening.

"T-Tyler, oh God," I whimper as he plunges into me, his thickness stretching and filling me completely. "It hurts."

"Relax, Lisa, "Tyler whispers soothing words in my ear and gently kisses the nape of my neck. "I'll take it slow, I promise."

As he eases himself back inside me, I focus on relaxing my muscles and letting him in. The initial discomfort fades into a slow, pleasurable burn as he rocks his hips back and forth. My grip on the bed sheets tightens as Tyler's pace quickens, each thrust more powerful than the last.

"Fuck me, fuck me, please," I moan, feeling my arousal growing with each movement. "Please, fuck me." My pussy is dripping wet with desire, and I can't help but beg for more. I continue to beg, my voice filled with desperation and need.

"Say my name, Lisa," he commands.

"Tyler."

"Louder."

"TYLER, T-Y-L-E-RRR!!!"

Tyler's hips are slamming against mine, and his hands are gripping my waist tightly. He knows exactly how to push me to the edge and keep me there, teetering on the precipice of pleasure and release. The sensation is overwhelming; I can't hold back any longer. With an uncontrollable cry, I shatter into a thousand pieces; my body convulses in his grip as waves of pleasure wash over me, leaving me trembling and gasping for breath. Tyler continues to drive into me relentlessly, prolonging my climax and drawing out every last drop of cum.

"I'm not finished yet," he growls, his voice laced with a primal need. Without hesitation, he pulls out of me and flips me onto my back, pinning my wrists above my head with one hand while the other guides his throbbing length back inside me.

. . .

I gasp at the sudden change in position, my body still pulsing with aftershocks from my previous orgasm. But Tyler shows no mercy, his movements becoming even more urgent and powerful.

My moans fill the room as he takes control, his dominance igniting a fire within me that I never knew existed. I surrender completely to him, giving into raw desire . Sweat glistens on his brow as he drives into me, chasing his own release. His grip on my wrists tightens as he thrusts deeper. My body responds eagerly to his dominant touch, my pussy lips clenching around him with each powerful stroke.

"Harder, Tyler!" I cry out. Tyler's eyes narrow with determination as he obliges; the bed creaks beneath us.

"Fuck, Lisa," he grunts, his voice filled with a mixture of need and satisfaction. "You feel so fucking good."

I arch my back and wrap my legs around his waist, allowing him to penetrate deeper, to claim me completely. The boundary between pleasure and pain blurs, and I revel in the delicious ache that courses through my body. His lips crash against mine, stealing my breath as he takes control of my mouth. Each kiss is fierce and possessive. His hands roam my body, gripping my thighs and my waist. His fingers find their way to my nipples, teasing and pinching them hard, leaving marks that will remind me of this moment long after it's over.

• • •

"Harder," I scream, craving the sweet release he can only give me. "Fuck me harder," I gasp, my walls clench around him, desperate for more of him.

Tyler's grip on my wrists tightens, his primal growls filling the room as he thrusts deeper, harder, pushing me closer to that edge.

"Come for me," he whispers in a voice filled with urgency and desire. "Let go, Lisa." And with those words, I surrender. We lie tangled together, hearts gradually slowing.

I blink awake as morning sunlight streams across my face. For a moment, last night felt like a dream. Then I become aware of the muscular arm draped over my waist, the warm body pressed against my back. I roll over to face Tyler, taking in his sleeping features. He looks younger like this, more at peace. My mind drifts back to the strange events of the night before. The urgent radio call, the way Tyler rushed me out before I could see what was happening. I need to know what's going on. I lean in and brush a soft kiss over his lips. His eyes flutter open, and he smiles drowsily at me.

"Good morning," I say.

He pulls me closer. "It is now."

His mouth finds mine in a slow, sensual kiss that makes my toes curl. I let myself get lost in it for a moment before pulling back.

"Tyler..." I begin hesitantly. "About last night, what was happening after I left?" His expression shutters. He sits up, the sheet falling to his waist. "I heard 'all clear.' Something was happening," I continue.

He shakes his head. "It was just a drill. Nothing you need to worry about."

I sit up, too, clutching the sheet over my chest. "I don't believe you. Please, tell me the truth."

His jaw tightens. "Drop it, Lisa. I mean it."

Frustration wells up inside me. I take a deep breath. He relaxes slightly and leans in to kiss me. "Thank you. Now come here..." I let him pull me back down into his arms, but I'm not giving up that easily. I'll get to the bottom of this, one way or another.

As soon as Tyler leaves, I spring into action. I urgently throw on my clothes and rush outside into the hazy morning air. The mist clings to my skin as I approach the venue where the event occurred last night. I scan the area for clues, walking around to the back, where I notice deep tire tracks in the muddy ground. But what really grabs my attention are the large, wet patches scattered throughout the dirt. Without hesitation, I crouch down and press my fingers into one of them -

completely saturated. My mind races with possibilities, but one thing is clear: something was definitely hosed down here. Just then, I hear voices getting closer and quickly stand up, ducking behind a nearby tree to hide from the approaching Navy personnel.

"I can't believe last night. Close call."

"I know, what a mess."

"Yeah, but there's gonna be hell to pay if this gets out."

My body is tense, and my mind races; my feet move before my brain registers it. I need answers. I sneak away and head for the newspaper office. As I dodge through the crowded streets, my mind pieces together the events of last night - Tyler's evasiveness, trying to rush me away, the voice on the radio, the cleanup. I quicken my pace, determined to uncover the truth. The stakes are far higher than I realized.

6

LISA

As the sun's golden rays spread over the crowd at Thanksville's town hall meeting, I navigate through the bustling sea of people. Ava, the Mayor's assistant, greets me with a broad smile and a knowing glint in her eye.

"Hey there, Lisa! Long time no see," she chirps.

"It feels like forever!" I reply with a polite grin.

I scan the familiar faces of my small town; something feels off. A group of men stands near the edge of the room, their hooded gazes and whispered conversations setting them apart from the rest of us. One man with slicked-back hair and piercing eyes studies everyone around him with calculated movements.

. . .

My attention is drawn to another figure in the room. James, one of the Navy SEALs in town for Captain Armstrong, is discreetly taking photos of the suspicious group with his phone; he clearly doesn't want to draw any attention to himself.

My pulse quickens. What is James up to? Why is he photographing these strangers? My heart races as I approach them, pretending to be interested in the conversations around me.

As I get closer, I strain to hear their words over the loud chatter of the crowd. Suddenly, a bad feeling washes over me. I recognize one of the men from a police report on the Valdez Cartel.

"Is everything alright?" someone asks me.

"Yes, I just need some air." I lie down smoothly. Trying to remain calm, I excuse myself and leave for fresh air. But my eyes never leave the group as they exchange brief words and disappear into the shadows. This is it – my big break. I have to gather as much information as possible without blowing it.

I burst out of the building, my eyes frantically scanning the streets for any sign of them. I see a flash of their jackets in the distance and start running, but they quickly disappear into the crowd.

. . .

Damn it, cursing under my breath. I must get to my office and dig through my files for anything I can find on him. The image of that cartel thug lingers in my mind. His presence can't be a coincidence; it has to be related to the recent event. My heels clicked urgently on the sidewalk. I have to find out everything I can about him.

Pushing open the heavy glass doors, I am greeted by the familiar scent of ink and paper, a momentary sense of calm before my adrenaline kicks in again. I quickly sit at my cluttered desk and begin typing furiously on my computer keyboard, searching for any files related to the elusive man I saw at the gathering.

Come on, come on, fingers flying across the computer keyboard as I search for any files related to the man I've seen at the gathering. I take a deep breath to steady my nerves as I scroll through the files, looking for anything to help me discover what he is up to.

Out of the corner of my eye, I spot a folder labeled "Sanchez, Miguel." Hands shaking, I open it. Inside are photos, rap sheets, and maps marked with locations. That's him. *Jackpot.*

I scan the documents, committing details to memory. Known cartel associates. Favorite weapons. Past assassination targets. Places he's been spotted. It can't be a coincidence that Sanchez showed up now. What is he planning here? And who has he come to kill?

•　•　•

The Mayor. It has to be. My breath catches as the pieces suddenly click into place.

Jaw clenched, I gather all the documents and stuff them into my bag. I have what I need to start putting the pieces together. But I need more, and I'm running out of time.

I rush from my office, heels clicking urgently down the hall. Outside, the sun is sinking below the horizon, casting the town in an ominous shadow. Somewhere out there, a killer is preparing for his deadly task.

7

TYLER

The vibrant rays of the rising sun illuminate Lisa's bare skin, casting a warm golden glow. I let my fingers glide over her body, savoring every inch, resisting the urge to pull her closer and stay in this blissful moment forever. But duty calls, and my team needs me.

"Tyler," she mumbles as she clung onto me. "Do you have to go?"

I gently kiss her forehead, wishing I could stay with her forever. "Yes, love. The briefing starts soon."

"Be careful," she murmurs as she stirs slightly, concern etched into her voice.

"I will," I assure her before closing the door behind me.

. . .

As I dressed in my uniform and gear, my heart aches at the thought of leaving her behind.

Lieutenant Philips stands at the front of the room, his posture rigid and eyes scanning the faces of each team member. James stands beside him, arms crossed and jaw tense.

The board behind them displays a photo taken by James during one of our covert operations - it's Miguel Sanchez, notorious assassin and member of the ruthless Valdez Cartel.

"Listen up," Philips begins, his voice cutting through the tension in the room. "This man is our target. We need to find out if there are any ties between him and the mayor, past or present."

I speak up, my mind racing through countless hours of investigation. "We've dug deep into Mayor Jackson's background and found nothing linking him to the cartel."

Phillips' eyes narrowed as he leaned closer to the photo, his finger jabbing at it with conviction. "This man is not just a random threat," he barks. "There's more to this than we know. He," pointing at the photo, "is here for a reason, and everything so far points to the mayor as his target."

A young Navy officer then steps forward, shuffling nervously on his feet. He clears his throat and speaks up, his voice shaking slightly. "Sir, while we were clearing up the bomb site, I saw a woman lurking around the back of the venue. She seemed suspicious."

Phillips' face tightens as he turns to face the officer."Did you get a description?"

"Mid-twenties, dark hair, about 5'5" tall," the officer replies, glancing down at his notes.

My heart skips a beat as I recognize that description all too well. It's Lisa.

"Damn it," Phillips cursed under his breath. I could see the tension in his jaw as he clenched it tightly. "Tyler, I told you to handle her." His tone left no room for argument or hesitation.

"Sir, she's not involved in any of this," I argue, but his tone remains cold and unyielding.

"SEAL, stay focused," Philips commands, his tone harsh and unwavering. "We can't have any loose ends jeopardizing our success. Keep a close watch on her."

I nod my agreement. As long as I long to shield Lisa from this world, I must do whatever it takes to keep her safe. Even if that means following her every move and risking the connection we've just forged. "Understood, sir," I say, though my heart struggles against the difficult task ahead.

. . .

I tail Lisa through the bustling streets, keeping my distance while never letting her out of my sight. Suddenly, a scruffy man appears at her side on a busy street corner. He leans in and whispers frantically, his breath hot and sour against her ear. "Excuse me, miss," he says, his voice quivering with urgency. "Did you know the Town Hall has hidden tunnels?"

Lisa's hand instinctively reaches for the pepper spray in her purse as she turns to face the stranger.

Good girl... I am ready to intervene.

"I'm sorry, who are you?" she asks, trying to keep her voice steady despite the fear flickering in her eyes.

"I hear things," the man continues, ignoring her question. "The mayor is involved with some pretty shady characters."

"Like who?" Lisa's reporter instincts kick in and she starts drilling him for more information.

But the man grows increasingly nervous, refusing to reveal any names."Can't say. Just be careful," he warns before quickly disappearing into the crowd.

. . .

I hear the low rumble of an engine drawing closer. My eyes narrow at seeing a black sedan creeping up behind her, its windows tinted and license plate obscured. Without thinking, I leap and run towards her, adrenaline pumping through my veins.

"Get down!" I yell, diving towards Lisa just as the car's tires squeal in acceleration.

Lisa staggers back, confusion etching her face as she turns to me. But before she can ask any questions, I grab her arm and pull her out of harm's way. The car narrowly misses us, crashing into a nearby lamppost instead.

"Tyler?" Lisa gasps, her body pressed against mine as we both fall to the ground. "What's going on?"

I hold onto her tightly, shielding her from any potential danger as I look over my shoulder at the wrecked car. "There's no time to explain," I reply. "Are you hurt?"

"I don't think so." she stammers, her voice trembling.

"Stay here," I leave Lisa behind and cautiously approach the car wreckage, my heart racing with adrenaline.

The smell of gasoline and broken glass permeates the air. My eyes scan for any signs of life, but all I find is a man slumped over the steering wheel, blood oozing from a fresh wound on his forehead. As I lean in to check for a pulse, I know I need to act quickly before the police arrives.

As I search the car for clues, my eyes land on an unusual dashboard feature. My instincts kick in, and I grab a pocket knife to pry open a hidden compartment. Inside, I find a set of tapes that could contain valuable information about the cartel's plans. I clench my fists, my mind racing with the weight of my discovery.

Lisa's inquisitive green eyes widened as she notices the tension on my face. "What did you find, Tyler?" she asks, curiosity burning through her tone.

"It's nothing," I lie, my hand gripping tightly onto the weighty tapes hidden in my pocket. With a quick excuse, I dash away from Lisa, police sirens getting closer. The recordings I found are burning a hole in my hand, and the implications weighing heavy on my mind.

As I race towards my destination, the streets blur past me, dodging pedestrians and cars until I reach our makeshift headquarters. Lieutenant Philips and the rest of our team are huddled inside.

"Tyler!" Philips exclaims upon seeing me burst through the door. "What happened? You look out of breath."

. . .

"I found these in a car that almost hit Lisa," I explain quickly, urgently handing over the tapes. "They could contain valuable intel."

"We need to decode these immediately," Philips says, his gaze locked onto the tapes with an intensity matching mine.

"I agree," I pant, still catching my breath from my mad dash. "But we'll need someone local to help us. There's no time."

"Find a local expert," Philips orders Derek. "We'll need their assistance,. "Derek," his voice hushed, "it's classified."

"Copy that, sir," Derek responds with a swift nod before disappearing.

Lisa's image lingers in my mind. The way she looked at me, the way her body felt pressed against mine – it's a craving I need to satisfy again. She is driving me crazy. Mad crazy. Obsessed crazy.

But now, she is in danger and I can't let anyone jeopardize what is mine.

I burst into her office and find her sitting at her desk with papers scattered around her."Lisa!" I said urgently, making my way towards her. "We need to talk."

. . .

"Tyler," she gasps, her eyes wide with surprise. "What are you doing here?"

"Protecting you," I reply firmly, standing close to her desk. "You're in danger, Lisa. You need to stop this investigation."

Her voice trembles slightly as she speaks again. "Excuse me? You can't tell me what to do." Despite her defiance, I can see the fear in her shaking hands.

I take her hand in mine, "Keeping you safe is all that matters."

"Tyler," she whispers, her gaze locked onto mine. "I –"

"Shh," I interrupt her, silencing her with a finger to her lips. "Don't say anything. Just let me keep you safe."

My hands slide around her waist, pulling her close until our bodies fit together perfectly. The heat from her body seeps into mine, and I can feel her heart racing in time with my own.

"Tyler," she gasps, her breath hot against my ear. "Please."

I grip her tighter, wanting to ensure she knows I'm here for her. "Please, what?" I growl, my voice low and husky.

•   •   •

"Make me yours again," she begs, her eyes searching mine with a desperate hunger that mirrors mine. "I need you."

My fingers tighten around her waist as I ask for confirmation. "Are you absolutely sure?" I ask, wanting to give her one last chance to change her mind.

"More than anything," she replies, her gaze never leaving mine.

Our lips crash together; I drink in every last bit of her, savoring the taste of her skin and her breath catching in her throat. She's everything I've ever wanted, everything I never knew I needed.

"Tyler," She moans as I deepen the kiss, holding onto me like I am her lifeline. "Don't let go."

"Never," I vow, knowing without a doubt that Lisa is mine – and I am hers. Nothing in this world can tear us apart.

EPILOGUE

TYLER

The moon's soft light filters through the bedroom window, and our breath's gentle rhythm fills the room as we lie together. Lisa traces her fingers over my broad chest. I can't believe how quickly we fell for each other, but every moment spent with her in my arms makes it clear that we are meant to be.

I explore every inch of her body, leaving her trembling with anticipation. This heat burns brighter with every passing moment. Lisa has surrendered completely to me.

"Tyler," Lisa's fingers dig into my shoulders, her nails drawing blood as she cries out in pleasure. Her body is a symphony of pleasure. I drink in the sounds of her moans, the taste of her breath mingling with mine. Each thrust is met with a gasp, a whispered plea for more. I hold nothing back, giving myself to her completely.

. . .

As we move together, our bodies become slick with sweat, and the air grows thick with heat. My every sense is consumed by the taste of her . Lisa's fingers claw at my back, her nails leaving fire trails in their wake. Her body arches beneath mine, aching for release.

"Lisa," I growl in response, the sound sending a thrill through her. Driven by an insatiable hunger, I push deeper and faster and plunge my cock deep inside her, claiming what's mine. Lisa's gasps and pleas for more only fuel my desire. We are both consumed, our minds and bodies wholly lost in the throes of passion until, finally, we collapse in a tangle of limbs and heavy breaths, completely spent and satisfied.

I lie next to her, my heart still pounding. Her head rests on my chest, her soft breaths sending warm waves through me. This is real, and I want it more than anything.

A contented sigh escapes her lips as she snuggles against me and I wrap my arms around her. The night is still around us, but I'm no longer lost in the darkness. With Lisa by my side, my pursuit is over.

SEALED LOVE CODE

A FORCED CLOSE PROXIMITY OTT
INSTALOVE ROMANCE

PROLOGUE

DEREK

The pungent odor of gasoline burns Tyler's nostrils as he scans the wreckage. Shattered glass litters the pavement, glinting in the moonlight. A man is slumped over the steering wheel, blood trickling from a gash on his forehead. Tyler reaches through the broken window to check for a pulse. Nothing.

He has to move fast. The sirens wail in the distance mean the cops would arrive any minute. Tyler rifles through the glove compartment, finding nothing but old receipts and gum wrappers. He pops the trunk - it is empty except for a spare tire and a few tools.

Damn it, slamming the trunk closed. He circles back to the front, leaning close to search every nook and cranny.

That's when he notices it - a discreet panel below the dash. Tyler grabs a screwdriver and pries it open. Nestled inside is a small bundle wrapped in cloth. Heart pounding, he unfolds it to reveal several tapes drives. Scrawled across the labels are dates and times.

Jackpot. These had to be what Lieutenant Phillips was looking for. This intel could be the key to uncovering the plans of the Valdez cartel.

Tyler slides them inside his jacket just as the first police car screeches around the corner and melts into the shadows, pulse racing as he clutches his precious cargo. He has to get these tapes to Lieutenant Phillips as soon as possible. The muffled wail of sirens fades behind him as he picks up his pace. Tyler can feel them pressed against his chest underneath his jacket, like a second heartbeat. The implications of what they contain weigh heavy on his mind.

Rounding the final corner, Tyler spots the nondescript building - their makeshift headquarters. He approaches the door and gives the secret knock - two quick raps followed by three slower ones. The door cracks open, and Tyler slips inside. The familiar faces of his team look up at him as he enters. Lieutenant Philips stands at the front, his arms crossed over his chest.

"Johnson, you made it back," Philips says gruffly.

Tyler reaches into his jacket and produces the tapes. "I found these, sir. Could be the intel we were looking for."

. . .

Philips' eyes lock onto the tapes, burning with intensity. He crosses the room and takes them from Tyler's outstretched hand.

"We need to decode them immediately," he barks.

"Yes, sir. We need to move fast. They just tried to run over Lisa," Tyler says.

Philips turns to me. "Hawkins, get these decoded ASAP. The rest of you, suit up."

I nod. "Understood, sir. "I'll locate a local specialist immediately, sir," I said confidently.

Philips' eyes narrow as he leans in closer. "This is highly classified information, SEAL," he hisses in a low voice. "I need you to handle it with the utmost discretion."

"Copy that, sir," I give Philips a sharp nod before turning on my heel and striding towards the door. I know exactly where to find the expertise we need - but can Emily Langston be trusted?

Failure is not an option. My mission is clear. And I will see it through, no matter the cost.

1

DEREK

I sit at the edge of the bed, watching her sleep, the soft rise and fall of her chest captivating me. The moonlight casts a soft glow on her face, highlighting the curve of her cheek and the arch of her nose. The sheets are tangled around her, leaving little to the imagination as she sleeps in just her lacy panties. I can't help but admire the full curves on display, wanting to touch, taste, and possess them all to myself. Her lips part slightly as she whispers something incoherent in her sleep, causing a jolt of desire to course through me. She looks so innocent and vulnerable.

I take a long breath and step closer. The gentle sound of her snores fills my ears, and I feel myself getting lost in their rhythm. Her body is curled up like a cat, one arm thrown over her eyes as she nestles deeper into the cushions. I can't resist leaning down to inhale her scent. My heart rate kicks up as I imagine what it would be like to have those luscious curves wrapped around me.

. . .

My eyes scan every inch of her – from the thick curls framing her face to the freckles sprinkled across her nose.

Shit. What am I doing?FOCUS on the mission!!

I inch closer to her, my hand gently pressing a compress with chloroform on her face. She stirs slightly but doesn't wake, allowing me to carefully reach for my duffle bag. I pull out a black hoodie and joggers, sliding them over her luscious body. With one swift motion, I grab her by the waist and lift her into my arms, carrying her to my car.

The night air is crisp against my skin as I make my way to the jeep parked nearby. She feels warm and soft in my arms, her body pressing against mine. I carefully place her inside before climbing in myself. Her scent fills the car, and I grip the steering wheel tightly as I navigate the quiet streets.

The cabin nestles deep in the woods, its wooden exterior blending seamlessly with the surrounding trees. I pull my car to a stop and cut the engine, plunging us into darkness save for the moonlight filtering through the dense branches over-head. Emily's head lolls against the seat. I scoop her up quickly, she's so damn light. As I carry her towards the front door, my heart's beating so hard it feels like it's trying to escape my chest. Her body is warm against mine, and she smells like vanilla.

Finally reaching the porch, I set her down, fumble for my

keys, and quickly unlock the door before ushering us inside and securing it behind us.

I light the woodstove and pour water into a pan and set it on the stove. Coffee will be ready when she wakes up; we have enough food to last a few days. I watch her as she moves. She stirs again and slowly opens her eyes confusion replacing the sleepiness in her features. She blinks rapidly, taking in our surroundings before her gaze returns to me. Fear flares within those brown depths.

"Wha-what's going on?" She tries to sit up but I push her gently back down.

"Don't worry," I assure her. "You're safe."

2

———————

EMILY

My arms tremble as I push myself up from the scratchy woolen blanket, taking in our surroundings. The cabin is small and rustic, with exposed wooden beams and a stone hearth crackling with fire. It's freezing outside; I feel the chill seeping through the thin walls. The scent of wood smoke and pine needles mixes with his manly smell, creating a blend that makes me queasy. I try to back away, my heart hammering against my ribcage as adrenaline courses through my veins.

"Wha-what's going on?" My voice trembles as I struggle against his grip.

"Don't worry," he says, his deep voice reverberating through my body. "You're safe."

Yeah, right.

. . .

He shifts on the hardwood floor, his broad shoulders filling the small space with an intimidating aura. I'm trapped; I can't move, think, or breathe. But I won't submit without a fight.

My chest heaves as I glare at him, my hands trembling angrily. "What do you want from me?" I snap. He towers over me, his piercing gaze taking every inch of my body. I realize I am wearing a hoodie and sweatpants.

He has dressed me. He has seen me… almost… N-A-K-E-D.

Without thinking, I grab the closest object – a lamp – and hurl it at him. He dodges it easily, but I keep throwing anything within reach. My mind races through escape plans while my body trembles with adrenaline.

"Stop fighting!" he bellows, catching one of my punches in his hand. "I am here to protect you!" he insists, his face contorting with frustration.

"Protect me?? You kidnapped me, you fucking asshole!!!" I scream, feeling tears of helplessness welling up in my eyes. "I don't need your damn protection. Let me go!"

He slams a box onto the bed and barks, "I need you to decrypt these tapes before anyone gets hurt." His urgency sends chills down my spine.

• • •

Hurt? What is he talking about?

"I must keep you safe and hidden until I get the all-clear," he adds, leaning against the wall, his muscular frame looming over me as he watches me closely. My captor. The man who has taken away my freedom.

"Couldn't you just ASK?"I shout, my anger giving me courage.

"We don't have time for that," he replies sternly. As he shifts, I glimpse the elaborate tattoos covering his arms, each telling a story of battles, losses, victories, and pain. A Navy SEAL. Damn, him! I can feel the heat of his skin burning into me. With trembling hands, I reach for the tapes and examine them.

"I need equipment ..." As the words tumble out of my mouth, he jerks open a door, revealing a dazzling array of state-of-the-art electronics.

"This is a matter of life and death," his tone is urgent. Sweat drips on my forehead as I realize the gravity of the situation.

No pressure...

3

EMILY

My eyes adjust to the faint light of a single lamp as I step into the dimly lit room. His strong jaw is clenched as he looks at me, his dark eyes flashing with concern for an instant.

Derek, his name is Derek, he said.

I resist the urge to fidget under his intense gaze, instead I take a deep breath squaring my shoulders and meet his stare.

I am good at this; this is why he brought me here. I remind myself. *If he wanted to hurt me he would have already.*

I pick one of the drives and sit at the desk, my hands shaking as I connect it to the laptop. The codes appear on the screen, and I furrow my brow in concentration as I begin to decode them. Derek leans closer to me, his body heat radiating off of him. I can feel the roughness of his skin and the hard planes of his stomach begging to be touched, igniting a fire within me. My fingers tremble as I press play, dread filling my chest at what I might find.

"I think I'm getting somewhere," I whisper, my fingers flying over the keyboard.

"Keep at it," Derek murmurs, his lips brushing against my ear. His voice is low and husky, sending shivers down my spine. Our breaths mingle as our bodies are barely an inch apart. Hours pass in what feels like minutes. The tension thickens with each passing minute until it is impossible to ignore. My chest heaves as I turn to face Derek, my heart racing with adrenaline.

"Ricardo Valdez," I say struggling to catch my breath. His jaw clenches at the name. "Who is he?" I ask urgently.

"He's the leader of the notorious Valdez cartel," he responds slowly, his voice filled with caution. "The man is ruthless and will do anything to get what he wants."

As Derek explains, I feel a knot form in my stomach. My mind races as I try to piece together all the information, desperate to understand what's happening. Derek reaches out to place a hand on my knee, gently squeezing it in reassurance. His touch sends quivers down my spine, and I force myself not to react. He doesn't know it, but he affects me - a strange mix of fear and desire that leaves me conflicted. As I frantically type on the keyboard, my heart races with urgency.

"Derek..." I start to say before his finger presses against my lips.

"Shhh," He grabs his gun from under the desk and motions for me to duck down.

"Wh...," his hand covers my mouth as he lifts a hidden door in the floorboards. Derek throws the laptop in and leads me in, his muscular form pushing me ahead and shielding me from danger. His touch is firm and possessive.

Heavy boots thudding against the wooden planks fill the room, echoing off its musty walls; someone is approaching, their footsteps getting closer and closer. The scent of fear mixes with the dampness of decaying wood, making my heart race as I hide in a corner. My body trembles against Derek's chest as he holds me tightly.

I hate that I need him, yet I crave him. My body aches for his.

"Don't move," he whispers urgently into my ear, his warm breath caressing my neck. My nipples harden under my clothes at his proximity, his hands pressed over my curves possessively. I can feel every muscle in my body relaxing, giving in to his dominance. "Stay here," he commands, giving me one last reassuring squeeze. "I'll draw him out."

. . .

I gulp, watching as he disappears into the darkness. The adrenaline rush makes me wet between the thighs. The smell of gunpowder lingers in the air, heightening my senses even more. Suddenly, I hear a loud crash followed by silence. My body tenses, but the adrenaline rush makes me feel alive. Slowly, I inch out of the hiding place and watch Derek tackle the man to the ground. Their bodies thrash against each other, muscles straining under their clothes. The sound of metal echoes in the night air as the man goes down. He turns towards me with heat in his eyes, chest rising and falling rapidly.

"Are you okay?" Derek's voice is rough and filled with concern.

I nod, still in shock from what just happened. But deep down, I can't deny the tingling sensation between my thighs at seeing Derek in action. "Yeah." I can't look away from those intense eyes or how his muscles flexed beneath his combats when he moves.

God, what is happening to me?

His eyes narrow as he leans towards me, and his grip tightens. "No one will ever lay a hand on you while I'm around," he says in a low, commanding voice. "You belong to me, Emily."

. . .

My heart pounds with fear and desire. I struggle against him, but my body yearns for his dominance.

"You don't own me," I retort, my voice wavering with desire. But deep down, I crave for him to take control. "I belong to no one," I force out through gritted teeth. Still, my body molds against him, and his intoxicating scent fills my senses - a mixture of sweat, musk, and dominance. In his arms, I feel safe.

4

DEREK

The assassin's body lies crumpled on the floor, a pool of blood spreading from his head. My chest heaves as adrenaline courses through me. My hands are still shaking from taking down that assassin. I look over at Emily; she stands frozen against the wall, eyes wide, fiery curls a mess, and her cheeks flushed. She's rattled but trying not to show it, stubborn as hell. I want to pull her into my arms, feel the softness of her skin, and inhale the scent of her hair.

I cross over and cup her face in my hands. "Are you okay?" She nods, breathless.

I pull her into me, one hand tangling in her curls. "No one will ever lay a hand on you while I'm around," I whisper. "You belong to me, Emily."

Her body trembles against mine. I want to crush her to me,

keep her safe in my arms. But there's no time. I release her and grab the satellite phone.

"Philips," comes the gruff voice.

"Sir, we need immediate exfil from the safe house." He responds with military precision, deploying a team for extraction.

"Copy that. Sending a team to your location."

I slam the phone down. We need to move fast. I turn back to Emily. Her eyes flash to mine. "What about the intel? I'm not done decoding-"

"Doesn't matter," I cut her off. "I'm getting you out of here."

"Don't be ridiculous; we have a job to finish. He is dead, isn't he?" She moves closer, challenging me. God, she smells good.

I harden my jaw. "My mission right now is to protect you. That's all that matters."

"I never asked for your protection," she snaps. But her eyes dart to my mouth.

· · ·

The air between us crackles. I grip her shoulders. "We're leaving. That's an order."

"You can't order me to do anything," she retorts, but her voice wavers. Our faces are inches apart now.

"The hell I can't." My heart pounds as I crush my mouth against hers. She responds with a hungry furious kiss. The world falls away for a moment, and it's just her body molded to mine. I'm lost in Emily.

Need courses through me as my body presses against hers, feeling her curves and softness. Her hands grip my neck, urging me closer, her kisses becoming more urgent. My hand runs down her back, over the fabric of the sweatpants, and over the roundness of her ass. I feel myself growing hard as I pull her closer, wanting more. With her body pressed against mine, there's no mistaking what I want. She meets my desire with equal fervor, allowing my hands to roam freely over her body. I slide one hand inside her sweatpants and feel her bare skin underneath. She gasps at the contact, and I feel her heat and wetness through her lacy panties. The scent drives me wild as I turn her around, my fingers tangling in her coarse hair until they reach their destination - a dripping pussy begging for attention. She moans as I slide a finger inside her, feeling the slickness and warmth enveloping me. Her head tilts back in pleasure.

I trail kisses down her neck, feeling the softness of her skin under my lips and her breasts rising and dropping as she breathes heavily. My hand moves lower, gently rubbing against her until I can feel the soaking wetness between her legs.

I increase the pressure, rubbing harder until her body shudders "Oh my God," she cries out.

"Not God, Emily. Just me."

I unzip my pants, revealing my eager erection to her. Her hands wrap around it, guiding me toward her awaiting entrance. It's reckless, it's dangerous. The team is going to be here any minute now. But I don't care. I enter her slowly, savoring every inch of her tight warmth.

"Emily, you have the tightest pussy."

When I sense that she's ready, I push forward with more force, causing her to cry out in pleasure. Her leg wraps around me, pulling me deeper inside her as we move together in rhythm. Our mouths meet in a hungry kiss as our bodies melt into each other and the intensity builds. I can feel her orgasm approaching, so I pull away to watch her face as it contorts with pure ecstasy. The sight pushes me over the edge, and I thrust hard into her before releasing deep inside.

I pull back, breathing hard. She looks up at me, lips swollen, cheeks flaming.

· · ·

"We need to move ," I say gruffly, picking up the gear. I try not to think about how perfectly she fits against me. How I never want to let her go.

She crosses her arms and lifts her chin. "I said I'm not going anywhere until I finish decoding those files."

Damn her stubbornness. Does she have a death wish?

"Later." I step toward her, our faces inches apart. "Right now, your safety is my mission. And I protect my mission at all costs."

Her lips part, cheeks flushing. Our eyes lock in a heated stare. A horn honks outside. The extraction team.

I grab her hand. "Now, let's go."

She digs in her heels. "No."

With a growl, I sweep her off her feet and toss her over my shoulder. She gasps and pounds against my back.

"Put me down!"

• • •

I carry her out the door. She can fight me all she wants. But I'm getting her out of here.

5

DEREK

The jeeps whip through the roads as we head to our makeshift headquarters. I help Emily; she stumbles on the floor as she steps out, her face pale with fear and anger. I steady her with a firm hand before leading her inside.

"Let's get you inside and find out what's on those tapes," I say gruffly, guiding her toward the tech room.

She quickly puts on a pair of headphones, still angry at me. She begins decoding the tapes, her fingers flying over the keyboard with expert precision. I still can't help but admire the view - fiery curls tumbling around her face, bottom lip caught between her teeth, billowing breasts peaking out from the hoodie.

"I've got something," Emily mutters. "Valdez is planning to take out the mayor ... something about ...the daughter ..."

· · ·

My gut twists. "When and where?"

"Something about…tomorrow…10am … civic center." Emily's eyes flash with anger. "He's doing it to punish the mayor for … something… something … Says here he…he plans to kidnap … during the attack."

I turn on my heel and stalk down the hall to Lieutenant Phillips' office. His brow furrows as he glances up from his desk, phone pressed to his ear. "Just got word. Mayor Jackson's been taken about an hour ago. Let's move," he says.

Wheels up in twenty. Valdez is going down.

EPILOGUE

EMILY

I awake to the feeling of Derek's strong arms wrapped around me, his muscular chest pressed against my back. The early morning sun filters in through the curtains of our beachside cottage, the sound of the waves a soothing melody.

Turning in his embrace, I smile up at his handsome face, relaxed in sleep. Reaching up, I traced the jagged scar on his cheek, a permanent reminder of the harrowing encounter with the Valdez cartel. We have faced such darkness together but come out on the other side stronger.

Derek's eyes flutter open, his piercing gaze meeting mine. "Good morning, Mrs Hawkins," he murmurs, his voice gravelly with sleep. He captures my lips in a deep kiss, his large hand trailing down my body sensuously. I sigh into his mouth, heat pooling in my core. His touch is gentle yet possessive. In his arms, I feel safe and desired, cherished in ways I never thought possible.

. . .

"Good morning, Mr Hawkins."

"You know," Derek whispers against my ear, his voice laced with desire. "The sun isn't the only thing that's hot this morning." A playful smirk dances across his lips as he pulls me closer, his body molding against mine.

With eager hands, I explore the contours of his body, tracing every scar and muscle that I have come to know so well. As his lips linger on mine, I feel the hunger in his kiss, the longing that burns between us. His hands roam over my body hungrily, tracing every curve and dip with possessive expertise that leaves me dizzy with desire. I surrender to his touch, the world around us melting into oblivion as he explores every inch of my skin with his skilled fingers. I am wet with desire.

"You are mine," he whispers.

"I am yours," I gasp, unable to resist the overwhelming desire coursing through me. My voice is hoarse and desperate as I offer myself to him, surrendering entirely to the consuming fire of our passion.

I have surrendered; I belong to him now. Together, we have found our love code.

SEALED BEYOND DUTY

A OTT AGE GAP FORBIDDEN ROMANCE

PROLOGUE

RICHARD

I slump in my chair, surrounded by stacks of documents and half-empty mugs of coffee. The flickering lamp above my head casts long shadows across the scratched surface of my desk. My hand runs over the creases on the report from Lieutenant Jake Philips outlining our covert operation in Thanksville. My eyes narrow as I stare at Philips' precise handwriting blurring before my eyes.

Thanksville.

The quaint town has become the stage for a clandestine dance between shadows, where danger lurks behind every corner. Intel had come in, whispering of a terrorist cell plotting an attack on Thanksville. To carry out our mission, I had to reach out to an old comrade, Mitchell Jackson.

The name takes me back twenty years to sand and blood and Mitchell's grin as we dragged each other out of hell. Now he's the Mayor there. I recall the reluctance in his voice when I explained the urgent need for our presence. Despite his reservations, he agreed. The team is undercover, blending in with the celebratory air of Captain Armstrong's 25th-anniversary commemoration. A town rejoicing in the memory of a fallen hero, yet the air is thick with the acrid scent of deceit.

Since our arrival, though, the whispers of danger turned into real, palpable threats. As I lean back in my old wooden chair, the creaking noise echoes the tension I feel in my body.

I rub my temples, Philips' words swirling in my mind. Three attempts already. Too clean, too close. And at the center of it all is one name that sends shivers down my spine – Valdez. It turns my stomach, even now. His cartel has grown into a hydra while we fought other battles, but their brutality remains unchanged.

The report in front of me details a connection between Valdez and Jackson. And now his pet assassin, Sanchez, stalks the city.

This is personal. A message for Mitchell. My jaw tightens. They won't succeed. I won't allow it.

I straighten in my chair, shoulders square. Has the legacy from our past missions finally caught up with us?

. . .

The town sleeps peacefully, unaware of the storm brewing within its heart. And in the midst of it all, my team and I stand as the last line of defense.

Valdez wants a war? He will have one.

1

RICHARD

My phone rings, jolting me awake. I glance at the clock—3:17 am. Never a good sign.

"Commander Dalton," I rasp into the receiver, my voice gravelly with sleep. It's Lieutenant Phillips on the line. His words turn my blood to ice. Mitch has been taken. Kidnapped from his own home in the dead of night.

A surge of adrenaline floods my body as I quickly process the information. He is a brother. Nothing will stop me from bringing him home if he's in trouble.

I bark orders to assemble the team. Moving in twenty. As I strap on my gear, adrenaline courses through my veins. Focus. Control. Getting Mitch back is all that matters.

. . .

The flight to Thanksville feels endless. Mitch's smile flashes through my mind. The day we became SEALs. His wedding. Hang on tight, brother. I'm coming for you.

I stride off the plane taking in the sleepy town. The armored vehicles and weapons—all just props. My mind is my true weapon, honed by years of training and sharpened by experience. And I will wield it mercilessly to find Mitch.

"Commander," Philips greets me.

"What's the status?" I ask him, my voice grim and determined. Philips quickly briefs me on the situation. I can tell by the look in his eyes that we both think the same thing: this is personal.

Mitch was taken while asleep; no sign of forced entry, just gone. It's strange but chillingly familiar. We approach Jackson's home. It is eerily quiet, almost unnervingly so except for the faint sound of a rooster crowing from afar.

A young woman is huddled on the front porch, trembling as if she is freezing even though it isn't particularly cold outside. Her face is streaked with tears, and her voice quivers when she speaks.

"They took him right from his bed," she clings to herself for warmth and comfort, "I should have been here."

. . .

I look at Philips. "Isabella Jackson, the Mayor's daughter," he says as if he could read my mind.

Mitch has a daughter? She can't be older than seventeen, nineteen at most ... he never ...

I see his warmth, his spirit in her eyes. She trembles as I introduce myself.

"Stay strong", I tell her. "We'll get him back".

Her lips part, she nods bravely, and then she throws herself into my arms. My vision blurs for a moment as I take this all in. Mitch's girl is sobbing into my chest, and the scent of her hair fills my senses. It's a mix of shampoo and fear, sweet and bitter at the same time. I can feel her soft, pillowy breasts pressed against my chest. So young. Curves as soft as butter.

She clings to me for dear life.

I cup her shoulders gently, pulling back just enough to look into her eyes. "I promise you, Isabella," I whisper, "we'll find your father and bring him home safe."

She nods, sniffling, her lower lip quivering as she pulls away from my chest and wipes her cheeks. Her eyes are wide with fear and relief as she takes a deep breath.

. . .

"Thank you... thank you so much," she manages.

My heart twists, wanting to comfort her even as duty calls me away.

I take a deep breath and approach where it all happened; my boots pound against the wooden floor as I storm into the bedroom, Philips close behind. My heart pumps with excitement and dread as I survey the scene. Stale air, fear, and desperation hang heavily in the air. The sheets are rumpled on the bed like Mitch struggled before he was taken. I see a strand of grey hair on his pillow - Mitch's. My hand trembles with the urge to crush something as I stuff it back into my pocket.

I turn away, jaw set. Mitch needs me. They will regret taking my brother. No one steals from a SEAL.

2

———————

ISABELLA

The word "kidnapped" echoes in my mind, clenching my chest and making it hard to breathe. The weight of those words presses down on me until I can barely breathe. Military personnel swarm around me in the house, their movements precise and focused. They all seem to be waiting for one man - Commander Richard Dalton. Dad's old comrade.

I see him arrive, his confident stride and commanding presence drawing everyone's attention. His salt-and-pepper hair stands out against the sea of uniforms, and his sharp features convey authority and determination. He is a force of nature, powerful and unstoppable. But it's his eyes that draw me in – steely blue pools that reflect the turmoil I am feeling inside. As I watch him, something inside me shifts, a fear giving way to an inexplicable desire.

When he turns and meets my eyes, everything else fades away. It's just him and I amidst the chaos of emotions.

Without thinking, I step towards him, my body responding to his magnetic pull. My fingers ache to trace the lines etched into his face from years of service, offering comfort without words.

His eyes widen, his surprise is evident in his mouth hanging slightly open.

"Isabella," he says, his voice deep and gravelly, vibrating through my body. "We're doing everything we can to find him." My voice trembles as I try to hold back tears, but his presence makes it impossible to keep up the facade of strength.

He reaches out a hand, hesitating before finally brushing a soft strand of hair away from my face. The touch is fleeting but sears through me, a jolt of heat that has no place here, not now. Yet, I crave more, yearning for the impossible.

"Your courage reminds me of your father," he says, his hand slowly dropping back to his side. But the warmth of his touch lingers on my skin like an unspoken promise.

I close my eyes, savoring the warmth that remains on my skin. My heart swells as I watch Commander Dalton in his element, barking orders and radiating authority. His muscles ripple beneath his uniform. At this moment, I am consumed by my feelings for him. I long to throw myself into the arms of this protector, to feel his passionate heart beating against mine.

. . .

"Bring him back to me," I whisper, my plea carried away by the cacophony that envelopes Commander Dalton once more. But I know he hears it, and I can see the determination burning in his eyes as he turns back to his task, muscles coiling.

I know he will stop at nothing to save those under his care. Fierce protectiveness and possessiveness radiates from within him. I am drawn even more to him.

I watch from a safe distance as he barks orders, his voice echoing with authority. The desire to be closer to him, a need to be claimed, to feel his intensity focused solely on me, is overwhelming. But for now, I wait and hope while keeping hidden the fire he ignites within me – a fire that only he can extinguish.

3

RICHARD

My ears buzz with the static of the decrypted message, adding to the tension in the room. Emily's fingers tap furiously on her keyboard, creating a rhythmic clack-clack-clack that fills the air. The screen illuminates her determined face, and I can't help but admire her tenacity under the circumstances. She's good—damn good—and it's a reminder of why we needed her on this op. Derek has done a good job finding her.

"Got it," she announces triumphantly, her voice cutting through the charged silence.

I lean over her shoulder, my muscles tense as I take in the coordinates flashing on the screen. A temporary Cartel hideout nearby. Every fiber of my body prepares for action, ready for the mission and rescue ahead.

· · ·

"They are keeping Mayor Jackson there," Emily states, meeting my gaze with urgency reflected in her eyes, "they are waiting to move him."

"Gear up," I bark out the orders, already visualizing our tactical approach and extraction plan.

The team bustles around me, checking equipment and securing ammo like the well-oiled machine we are. My hands move automatically, familiar with the routine after years of training. But as I double-check my gear, Isabella's face flashes in my mind—the curve of her lips, the warmth of her touch when she handed me her father's favorite watch, entrusting me with more than just a timepiece. It was a promise, an unspoken plea for his safe return.

Guilt tears through my chest, clawing at every fiber of my being. My duty calls, but the inferno that ignites within me when Isabella is near lures me towards her like a moth to a flame. I can't give in to these desires; I have a mission to fulfill. I can't: she could be my daughter. She is Mitch's daughter.

But the pull only grows stronger, threatening to shred the carefully constructed walls of my disciplined existence. The mere thought of her sends a burning ache coursing through my veins. I want her with an insatiable hunger. God help me; I crave her with every ounce of my being.

. . .

I push it down, bury it deep inside, locking it away in a dark corner of my mind. This mission is about Mitch, about bringing him home safely. It has to be. But even as I try to convince myself, the searing heat of Isabella's eyes sears into me like a branding iron, reminding me of the forbidden temptation that threatens to consume me. I need her like oxygen to breathe.

I snap out of my thoughts as one of my men shouts, "Commander?"

I quickly respond, strapping on my bulletproof vest and checking the ammunition in my weapon. Each click and snap of gear is a ritual that brings me back to the present moment.

We move forward like ghosts under the cover of darkness, our shadows blending seamlessly into the night. My boots pound against the ground with a steady rhythm, matching the rapid thumping of my heart. Every step takes us closer to Mitch, closer to fulfilling our duty.

And with every step, there's a growing, persistent ache - a longing for someone who has no place in this mission. Isabella. Her name alone stirs up warmth and danger, coiling tightly around my chest and settling into the pit of my stomach.

Stay sharp, I chastise myself, forcefully pushing aside the distracting thoughts. *Mission above all else.*

• • •

As we approach the hideout, the moon casts an eerie glow over the building, making it seem like a menacing creature waiting to strike. This is it - time to bring Jackson home. Time to bury any forbidden desires that have no place in a SEAL's heart.

"Positions," my team springs into action as I whisper into the comms. Each man takes his designated position, every movement precise, every breath measured. We're ready. For the fight, for the rescue. For the duty that overshadows all else.

At this moment, I am Commander Richard Dalton, SEAL to the core. And yet, somewhere deep within, where discipline meets desire, I make a silent vow. Once this is done and Mitch is safe, I'll confront the conflict raging within me. Isabella's touch, her presence, has pierced the armor I've worn for so long.

But not now. Now, there's only the mission. Only duty. And that's all there can be.

4

RICHARD

Thick raindrops pelt our tactical gear as we approach the cartel temporary hideout, creating a slick layer on the dense foliage around us. My team and I move like a well-oiled machine, each step calculated and fluid as we close in on the compound. The pounding of rain and loud crashes of thunder are drowned out by the rumbling beat of my heart, racing faster with each passing second. I wipe the sweat from my brow, my hand shaking slightly as I survey the compound through my high-powered binoculars. In the southeast corner, I spot Jackson tied up and gagged.

With precise hand signals, I direct my team to their designated positions. We move with silent precision, our movements trained and practiced as we breach the perimeter. The shouts of the cartel members and the whizzing sound of bullets only add to the chaotic atmosphere as we engage in a fierce firefight. Every muscle in my body is coiled and ready for action as we work together to rescue our brother.

· · ·

Through the haze of gun smoke, I glimpse my seals pushing forward relentlessly with me. The thrill of combat courses through me, almost masking the coppery taste of anticipation on my tongue. Victory is within reach – all we have to do is take it.

We burst into the dimly lit room, gun drawn and ready for a fight. My sharp eyes quickly locate Jackson, bound and battered in a chair. Without hesitation, I rush to his side and start cutting through the ropes with my trusty rescue knife. He winces as I free him, but his fierce expression tells me he's ready for revenge.

"What took you so long?" he growls, standing up with my help. I grab him and pull him close, my eyes scanning the room.

"Isabella," he pleads, "Isabella."

"She's safe," I reassure him. "Let's get you out of here." We find ourselves surrounded by sweaty, armed men shouting in Spanish, trying to regain control of their situation as we exit swiftly. The sound of a gun cocking snaps my attention to the man standing behind me, a weapon aimed at my back. Time seems to slow as I duck and roll to the left, just as the bullet grazes my shoulder. My SEAL training kicks in, and I immediately return fire, taking out several enemy cartel members before seeking cover behind a crate.

·　·　·

The smell of sweat, blood, and fear fills the air as we engage in an intense firefight. The gunfire echoes off the walls, each shot missing its mark by mere inches. Adrenaline is running through my veins . With one final glance at the compound, we retreat into the darkness, leaving behind the lingering shadows of combat.

5

ISABELLA

The Commander and the team have been away for what seems like ages.

Commander … I whisper and immediately feel guilty for thinking about Richard instead of my father's safety. Is he okay? Is he even alive? Richard has left some men to stand guard at our home.

Suddenly, the door creaks open, and I hear my name being called. "Father!" I shout, running towards the entrance. My eyes widen with a mix of relief and concern as I take in the sight of him - battered and bruised but alive. "Father," I breathe, tears welling up in my eyes.

He opens his arms and pulls me into a tight embrace. "I'm okay sweetheart," he murmurs, his voice a soothing balm against the horrors he must have faced. "I'm home."

• • •

As we step inside, the door closes behind us and I see Commander Dalton standing in the foyer. His eyes meet mine; he kept his promise and brought him back to me.

"You need to get checked out, Mitch," Richard says, addressing my father, who reluctantly agrees.

The room is filled with silence, heavy and thick, like it has a life of its own. We are finally alone. I press my back against the cold wall, trying to ground myself in reality. But then Commander Dalton approaches me, his body radiating warmth that seeps through my flimsy dress.

His intense gaze meets mine, setting off an inferno in my chest. It's the same unwavering look he gives his SEALs, but now it's softened and directed solely at me. He speaks my name like it's a sacred oath, and every nerve in my body responds to the sound of it.

"Isabella," he whispers again, enunciating every single syllable, and I feel like I'm drowning in his voice. My heart beats wildly .

The space between us vanishes as he steps closer, his broad chest nearly touching mine, our bodies so close that I can feel the warmth of his breath mingling with mine.. He hesitates, a brief war waging behind his eyes. Duty versus desire. But then, as if driven by a force greater than himself, he lowers his head toward me. His lips find mine in a kiss that ignites a firestorm of sensation, melting away the last remnants of restraint.

I reach up, fingers tangling into his short-cropped hair, the salt-and-pepper strands a stark contrast to my own dark locks. The texture is rough under my touch. His arms encircle my waist, pulling me impossibly closer, sealing the infinitesimal gap that had separated us. His touch is firm and protective—an unspoken promise that here, in his embrace, nothing could ever harm me.

Our kiss deepens, and I taste the raw intensity of his longing —the pent-up passion of a man who has always put duty first, now teetering on the brink of surrender. Each caress of his lips sends shivers down my spine; each breath he exhales against my skin fuels the flames higher.

He's holding back, I can tell. Even now. Yet, beneath that control, I sense the simmering heat. His hands roam over my back with a restraint that belies the fierce desire I feel resonating from his every move.

My pulse races, my body humming with a need I've never known before. In his arms, I'm no longer just Isabella Jackson, the Mayor's daughter—I am the woman who has awakened something primal in a man who exudes authority and power. And as the kiss slows I know this is only the beginning.

There's no turning back now. Not for him. Not for me.

6

RICHARD

Mitch's face is swollen and bruised, his body trembling as he struggles to sit up. I feel anger as I stare at him, knowing in my gut there's something more to this. He is hunched over, his hands clasped together, a picture of guilt and fear. But above all, I need answers about Isabella. My hands grip the edge of the table tightly as I stare down at him, my jaw set and eyes hard.

"Did you have any idea Valdez was after you?" I growl, my fists clenched at my sides.

"Rick," he says, his attention entirely on me now.

"Tell me everything," I demand, my tone brooking no argument.

. . .

"My Anna..." His words came out in a rush, his voice thick with emotion, remembering his late wife. "Anna was engaged to Valdez when we met," he confesses, his tone gravelly and pained.

"We fell in love," he continues, his fear and stress evident in his husky voice. "She left Ricardo and came to me after she found out she was pregnant."

"Elena," I say. "Operation Ruby."

"Yes, Elena Montoyez," Mitch nods, his expression pained as he remembers her. He runs a hand over his face, wiping away the memory of her name on his lips. "I gave her a new identity," he says, his tone heavy. "Helped her raise Isabella as my own."

My mind reels at this revelation - Valdez's daughter. It all makes sense now.

"Jesus," I mutter, unable to find any other words. "This changes everything," shaking my head and taking it all in. Valdez is never going to rest.

He meets my gaze with guilt in his eyes. "I should have told you," he continues, his voice strained.

• • •

"You damn well should have! You could have gotten all of us killed!" I yell, slamming my hand on the table, fighting the urge to lunge at him.

Mitch meets my gaze, his eyes clouded with pain. "Belle isn't safe here anymore," he says.

I nod solemnly, feeling the weight of that truth. Protecting Isabella is all I can think of.

"I'll take care of her; I love her." I declare firmly, my voice rough with emotion. "I'll do whatever it takes."

7

ISABELLA

I have been waiting in my bedroom for father to come back from the hospital. Too many people in the house right now. I seat quietly in my bed, the feel of Richard's kiss still on my lips. I want him to be my first and my last.

"Isabella," a whisper behind my door. I open it and Richard is standing there, his intense gaze locked onto me.

"Isabella," his voice booms like thunder, sending shivers down my spine. His possessiveness is evident in the way he says my name.

"Rick," I breathe out, savoring the sound of his name on my lips like a promise.

Closing the distance between us, he steps closer until there is no space left to separate us, his calloused hands gentle as they frame my face. My body responds to his touch, the fire within me reignited by the forbidden desire that has been growing since our first glance.

The door closes behind him.

My heart pounds like a wild animal trapped inside a cage. I lock eyes with him, the intensity of his gaze pulling me in like a magnet. I read the silent vow in them, a pledge that extends beyond duty. Here, it's just us—no rules to keep us apart.

He leans in close and whispers my name, "I want you, I need you, I crave you," the words laced with a raw need that resonates within my soul.

Without hesitation, I rise on the tips of my toes to meet him, my hands exploring every ridge and muscle of his broad shoulders. The strength and power under his skin are palpable, and I crave the heat from him.

Our lips collide in a burst of pent-up desire, the force of our longing palpable. His mouth moves over mine with urgent hunger, and I respond in kind, my need driving me forward. His tongue traces the edges of my lips, seeking entrance, and I eagerly grant it.

As we deepen the kiss, my body melts into his like two puzzle pieces finally fitting together. His hands roam over me possessively, exploring every curve and dip as though he's memorizing my body. I cling to him, tangling my fingers in his salt-and-pepper hair as he lifts me easily and carries me towards the waiting bed.

With each step he takes toward the bed, I feel the layers of resistance shedding away. This is the culmination of every stolen glance, every unspoken word heavy with meaning.

"Rick ...I never...done it, "I confess.

"I'll be gentle baby," he responds by trailing kisses along my skin, his touch gentle and reverent. But I don't want gentle-ness – I want him to take me without hesitation.

"No, take me, don't hold back," I plead with him.

"Are you sure?" he asks.

I nod with hunger, unable to wait any longer. Without any doubts or reservations, his hands explore every inch of my body with devotion and passion. At this moment, he isn't just taking my body but also my heart that's been waiting for him all along.

"Mine," he groans, a mantra etched into the rhythm of our joining.

. . .

"Yours," I gasp, the truth ringing clear and undeniable.

His hands move lower, trailing over my hips and thighs before settling on the hem of my dress. He tugs it upwards, slowly revealing more of my flesh to his touch, his fingers grazing along my silky skin. The dress pools around my waist, leaving me exposed before him. My heart hammers against my chest as I watch him take me all in, drinking me in like a man possessed. His eyes travel to every inch of my body fueling his desire for me more.

Heat pools between my legs, and his touch is like lightning on a rainy day, a sudden, unexpected storm that sends shivers down my spine. His lips find the pulse point at the base of my neck, sucking gently while his teeth scrape against my skin – a perfect mix of pain and pleasure that sends shockwaves through me. His tongue swirls around, lapping up beads of sweat as they form on my skin.

With a growl, he crushes his lips against mine once more while his hands cup my ass cheeks possessively. I feel him nudge my thighs apart, and I oblige without hesitation. As he enters me with one thick finger, I cling to him tighter, wanting more of this man who claims me so effortlessly.

My moans echo off the walls, mingling with his groans as he pushes deeper, stretching me. Each thrust sends waves of pleasure through my body. His kiss is fierce; his teeth graze my lower lip, drawing blood and leaving a tiny sting as he tastes it greedily. He grows bolder, biting down harder as he plunders my mouth. His other hand has found my breast, rolling the nipple between his thumb and forefinger, causing me to arch into him. I gasp at the onslaught of sensations bombarding my body, unable to contain the noise as the world around us disappears. His breath mingles with mine, hot and heavy against my neck, while his fingers dance inside of me. I can feel his intense desire pulsating against my core.

His kisses trail down my jawline to the hollow of my throat, leaving a trail of wetness and desire in their wake. His lips graze my collarbone, sending shivers across my skin. He pulls back to look at me, eyes blazing with lust and possession as he watches himself sink into me further.

"You're perfect," he whispers against my skin before claiming my lips again, his tongue teasing mine and exploring every inch of my mouth. His hands find my buttocks again and press me further into him as he claims what is his. I gasp at the feel of his rough palm against my bare opening and shiver involuntarily.

"Take me, Rick, take me, please, "I plead. He teases my entrance slowly at first. My breath catches in anticipation of what's to come as his huge cock slips through my wetness and finds its target. I can feel his big hard cock pounding, pinning me beneath him. He stays still for a moment as I adjust to the unfamiliar sensation. He's bigger than I expected, thick and hard, but it feels so right.

His muscular body moves with a fierce urgency like a predator who finally finds its prey. Then, with a low groan, he drives himself deep into my willing body in one powerful thrust.

The bed creaks and moans under our combined weight, the springs straining as the headboard slams against the wall with each forceful entry. He buries himself up to the hilt, filling me completely, claiming me.

His chest hair tickles my soft skin, and I feel every ripple of muscle beneath him as he takes control. The sensation of his thick cock stretching me is both exquisite and overwhelming, sending waves of pleasure coursing through me.

"You feel so good," he whispers against my neck, his hot breath sending shivers down my spine.

Slowly, almost tortuously slow, he begins to move within me - retreating slightly, then plunging back in again. His balls slapping against my bottom with each powerful stroke send shockwaves of pleasure through me. With every thrust, I feel him deeper inside of me, claiming me as his own. His hips sway with each powerful movement, grinding against mine as if he can't get enough.

His hands roam to my breasts, pinching and rolling my nipples between his thumbs and forefingers while his other hand grips the nape of my neck possessively.

. . .

"You taste so fucking good," he murmurs between ragged breaths.

I moan loudly, throwing my head back into the pillows as I feel him thrust deeper inside of me. His beard scrapes against my neck, sending shivers down my spine. His taste is addictive, his touch possessive. I can feel every inch of his huge body moving against mine like a rhythm we've danced to for years.

My breathing hitches when he strokes me just right, hitting that spot deep within me that sends lightning bolts straight to my core. I grip onto the sheets beneath us, "Rick, R-I-C-K, oh my G-O-D."

"You are mine, baby," and I feel myself filling with his juice, "Now and always."

EPILOGUE
RICHARD

I stand tall looking at my crisp naval uniform hanging in the closet, my hand unconsciously running over the pinned medals. Each represents a battle fought and won, but none compare to the triumph I feel when I look into Isabella's eyes. Five years have passed since she became my world, my wife. Her touch still sends shivers down my spine, igniting a fire within me that only she can quench with her hands.

"Rick," her voice whispers like a siren, pulling me away from my thoughts.

"Isabella," I respond, my voice low. Nothing compares to the weight of her love-filled gaze, tinged with something new—a spark of creation.

She rests her hand on the swell of her belly, our future pressing against her skin. I place my palm over hers, feeling the life we've created together stir beneath our touch. A primal urge to protect them surges through me, and I know I would burn the world to ashes if it meant keeping them safe.

"Do you feel that?" Isabella's voice is soft, her dark hair framing her face like a shield. "Our little one knows you're here."

"Every kick, every movement—I feel it all," I reply. My voice is filled with wonder as I lean down to press a kiss just above where our unborn baby dances.

Her soft hand trembles as it reaches for my face, and I feel her eyes searching mine. "Promise me," she pleads. "Promise me you'll always be there."

I take her delicate hand in mine as I squeeze her fingers gently, "Always," I vow, sealing my promise with another kiss on her forehead. "You are my world, my one and only, Bella. You and our child—my heart beats for you."

She reaches up to cup my cheek, her touch warm and grounding. At this moment, I feel more anchored than any command could ever make me feel. She rests her head against my chest, and I protectively wrap my arms around her. This is my mission now – to love and care for my family above all else. Beyond these walls, the world continues to turn, Valdez our shadow, but for this moment, nothing else exists.

· · ·

Just Bella, our child, and the unbreakable bond that seals us beyond duty.

GET YOUR FREE EBOOK

AUTHOR'S NOTE

Thank you so much for reading **Navy SEAL Hunks**.

I hope you enjoyed the stories. A review would be much appreciated as it helps other readers discover the story. Or a few stars perhaps - the more the better ;-) !

Thank you.

ABOUT THE AUTHOR

Laura (L.A.) Mariani is a best selling author of Short & Steamy Romance | Where Alpha Males Meet Fierce Heroines for Sweet Endings, your go-to author for captivating romance tales that will sweep you off your feet and keep you on the edge of your seat!

When Laura is not weaving stories of love, desire and suspense, you'll find her exploring the vibrant streets of London, drawing inspiration from its hidden corners and bustling markets, or strolling through the charming streets of Paris, savoring street food in Rome, or relaxing on a sun-kissed beach in Bali, her journeys fuelling her creativity and infuse her stories with wanderlust.

You can also follow her on

𝕏 x.com/PeopleAlchemist
instagram.com/lauramariani_author
facebook.com/lauramarianiauthor

www.ingramcontent.com/pod-product-compliance
Lightning Source LLC
Chambersburg PA
CBHW070608170726
48291CB00003B/750